"What hen-witted gibberish is this?" he raged.

In three strides he had crossed the room and grasped her by the shoulders. "Do you honestly think me capable of dallying with innocents? If anyone is in danger, it is you. You seem a prime piece to warm a man's bed."

Rosanna's heart was pounding but she refused to back away from him. "Remember, it is only the fair-haired chits you favor. You made that most clear!" Rosanna tossed her dark locks. "I have nothing to fear from you."

"I wouldn't be so sure!"

The dangerous glitter in his eyes gave warning, but before Rosanna could put her hands up against his chest to ward him off, he yanked her into his arms. Hard lips descended to plunder her mouth. It was so quick she had no time to raise her defenses. At the touch of his lips, an answering fire blazed up within her and for a moment her mouth softened and clung to his in willing surrender. Then she stiffened. She had given her kisses to a rake once before. . . .

Dear Reader:

As the months go by, we continue to receive word from you that SECOND CHANCE AT LOVE romances are providing you with the kind of romantic entertainment you're looking for. In your letters you've voiced enthusiastic support for SECOND CHANCE AT LOVE, you've shared your thoughts on how personally meaningful the books are, and you've suggested ideas and changes for future books. Although we can't always reply to your letters as quickly as we'd like, please be assured that we appreciate your comments. Your thoughts are all-important to us!

We're glad many of you have come to associate SECOND CHANCE AT LOVE books with our butterfly trademark. We think the butterfly is a perfect symbol of the reaffirmation of life and thrilling new love that SECOND CHANCE AT LOVE heroines and heroes find together in each story. We hope you keep asking for the "butterfly books," and that, when you buy one—whether by a favorite author or a talented new writer—you're sure of a good read. You can trust all SECOND CHANCE AT LOVE books to live up to the high standards of romantic fiction you've come to expect.

So happy reading, and keep your letters coming!

With warm wishes,

Ellen Edwards

Ellen Edwards
SECOND CHANCE AT LOVE
The Berkley/Jove Publishing Group
200 Madison Avenue
New York, NY 10016

Second Chance at Love

REGENCY

THE ARDENT PROTECTOR
AMANDA KENT

A
SECOND CHANCE AT LOVE
BOOK

THE ARDENT PROTECTOR

First edition published March 1983

First printing

"Second Chance at Love" and the butterfly emblem are trademarks belonging to Jove Publications, Inc.

Printed in the United States of America

Second Chance at Love books are published by
The Berkley/Jove Publishing Group
200 Madison Avenue, New York, NY 10016

CHAPTER
One

ROSANNA GLANCED UP from the estate's book. Hobart's ponderous tones penetrated from the entry hall to the study where she was checking the bailiff's figures. "Lady Wythe left instructions that she is not at home to callers, sir," she heard the butler announce in his most quelling voice. "If you wish, you may come back tomorrow. Perhaps she might receive you then."

"Hell and damnation, man, stand aside," snapped an authoritative voice that sounded more used to commanding regiments in the Peninsula than arguing with an aged retainer. "I have ridden hell-for-leather to get here. I have no intention of returning tomorrow or any other time. Inform your mistress that I am here! Be quick about it, or I shall go and search for her myself."

Rosanna's usually sunny eyes turned a stormy gray when she heard the raised voices. Apparently the snippets of gossip flying for a fortnight that Giles's cousin would call were true. Rosanna sighed. She'd best receive him briefly now. Delaying wouldn't make the scene any more bearable. Perhaps if her father-in-law knew his plot had failed, he would leave her alone.

Rosanna shook her head grimly, recalling the rumors of Squire Wythe's plan that had reached her. With his pockets empty and the duns pounding on his door, he'd decided to see if Giles's cousin Wilbert could woo her

and her fortune into the family coffers a second time.
She raised her chin stubbornly. Squire Wythe was a fool
if he thought she'd agree to marry another member of
his family. One husband of Giles's rakish stamp had been
more than enough! She wished herself rid of the entire
Wythe clan. Her hand returned the quill steadily to its
stand, but there was an uneasy tightness in her throat as
she rose to her feet. She automatically smoothed her long
dark hair, then shook out the folds of her gown. Yanking
the bellpull, she summoned Hobart to bring the stranger.

The carved door to the study opened. "Madam"—the
butler creaked low in a bow—"this gentleman is—"

"Yes, I know." Rosanna forestalled him with a wave
of her hand. "I shall receive him."

She folded her hands calmly in front of her black
widow's weeds and met the caller's look coldly. He was
a bit of a surprise. Giles had been tall, but this man
topped him by several inches. He carried this height well,
but lacked the pantherlike grace of her dead husband.
The stranger strode into the room rather than walked. It
was a powerful but not an elegant stride. Rosanna eyed
his expensively cut champagne riding breeches and velvet
coat, noticing how the smooth lines were ruined by his
saddle-hardened muscles, which even Weston's master
hand couldn't conceal.

She wondered where Giles's cousin got the blunt to
indulge in such fashions of the first stare. The Wythe
clan was never known to be plump in the pockets. Probably he resided deep in dun territory, like the rest of
them. Yet something about the man jarred with this con-
demnation, she decided, her gaze flicking over him a
second time. Maybe it was the way the arrogance of his
chiseled features was softened by the ash-brown hair
curling at the back of his neck, or by the lines carved

by laughter around his blue eyes. No, he didn't have the usual look of a Wythe, but, as she'd discovered to her sorrow, looks rarely bespoke the truth.

Noticing how the stranger raised a sardonic brow at her inspection, she nodded. No doubt he was usually the one who ran a speculative eye over a woman's figure, not vice versa. An intrigued smile curled the man's firm lips as their eyes locked. Indeed, he had the look of a rake. Best let him learn right now that he was not dealing with a schoolroom miss who could be easily put aflutter by his undeniably appealing smile.

Rosanna's hands twisted tighter as she remembered a similar smile on Giles's face that had caused her foolish heart to turn over. Look what trouble and heartache that had brought! Yet all the painful memories and brave words couldn't protect her from responding to the man standing before her.

Determined not to reveal the unsettling effect his broad shoulders and laughing eyes were having on her heartbeat, she commented curtly as she crossed the room toward him, "I had heard you were a dandy, sir, and indeed your address is more impressive than the usual fops who visit our local assemblies. But it won't do you any good." She sat down behind the tea service and removed the quilted cozy. "Will you take tea? Perhaps a brandy would be more consoling for a rejected proposal?"

The man ran a hand through his hair in seeming confusion. "My proposal? I didn't come to—"

"Oh, is it to be wooing?" she interrupted, handing him a cup of the fragrant brew. "How gallant! I vow you Wythes are always handy at turning a pretty phrase. It's a pity your actions aren't as attractive," she added harshly, remembering her shock at finding her husband in bed with his bit of muslin a scant week after they were wed.

She pursed her lips as the painful memories returned. It was then she'd discovered that Giles had riveted himself to her for no other reason than that her land marched with his. How the village tabbies must have laughed to hear that she, a Millbourne, had fallen for his honeyed lies. Rosanna gave herself a shake. All that was in the past now. One of Napoleon's musket balls had resolved the problem a good fourteen months ago.

"What hen-witted gibberish is this about proposals and wooing? Lady Wythe, I don't understand your meaning, and you certainly don't understand mine." The man cocked a raffish eyebrow at her. "As the scheming mamas of the *ton* will tell you, I'm not the wooing kind. As for being shackled to a wife, I'd rather not. Life is, ah, too interesting to bother with setting up a nursery."

"I declare, is it to be a *carte blanche*, then? That shall not pour my fortune into your empty pockets."

"Tut, tut, milady," he admonished with a casual flick of his finger. "As your guardian, I find such words unbecoming."

"As my *what?*" Rosanna echoed blankly.

"Your guardian. That is why I—"

She stood up abruptly, stilling his words. "Rubbish! No man is my guardian, least of all a Wythe. Just because you are Giles's cousin gives you no leave to claim such a relationship! Pray tell my father-in-law that the gossipmongers have been talking. I know of his scheme, and it won't work. I have no intention of wedding you or anyone else. The Millbourne lands and fortune will stay in my hands. You, sir, can go to the devil!"

"No doubt I will at some time, but not today," he remarked, pointedly ignoring her motion of dismissal.

Rosanna became even more vexed when she noticed

how his lips curled into an amused smile as he watched her small foot tapping impatiently. She stopped the motion instantly and wondered how much plainer she could make herself. Even if he were quite the most attractive man she'd seen in a vast age, a fact she grudgingly had to admit, he was still Giles's cousin, and she wanted nothing more to do with any of that family!

When she said nothing else, the man made her a formal bow. "No doubt we should begin again, Lady Wythe. There is some misunderstanding here. I'm not your husband's cousin, whoever that dandified chap might be."

"Do you mean you aren't Sir Wilbert? But they said he was coming to call and—" She stopped, disliking the foolish sound of her words. If he wasn't Giles's cousin, what was this guardianship nonsense he was mumbling about?

"Who are you, then?" Rosanna demanded, trying to straighten out her confusion. "And what gives you call to claim some absurd relationship where none exists?"

"Frankly, the law insists that it is my right—and, unfortunately, my responsibility." His look clearly indicated that he saw the storm brewing in her eyes. "Before we come to fisticuffs, milady, let me make myself known to you. I am Chandler Hartwick, Earl Leighton. I believe you were acquainted with the late earl, my father."

Rosanna's eyes widened. So this was Leighton's wild son, she thought, looking more closely at the man towering in front of her. She recalled the late earl's long-winded lamentations on the rakish life led by his only son. Her father, knowing well of his old friend's fanatical puritanism, at first tried to defend the man's heir. But he stopped when the rumor mill continued to carry frequent tales of young Hartwick's amorous exploits.

Shaking her head, Rosanna decided that Chandler wasn't at all what she expected. To her mind, a rake should be elegantly suave, with world-weary lines of dissipation about the eyes—and preferably dark, like the romantic Lord Byron. Or, she couldn't help but add, like Giles.

This man hardly fit that picture. Clear blue eyes returned her gaze as she continued to study him. He was certainly no drawing-room dandy. His sun-streaked hair and tanned skin bespoke hours spent in the open. He looked as if he would be more at home outdoors on a hunting field or...

Outdoors! Now she remembered. Chandler Hartwick, hero of the Peninsula Wars. His daringly bold exploits on the battlefield were as famous as those with the ladies. Grudging acknowledgment of his bravery constituted the only kind words she remembered the late earl ever having said about his son. Well, she supposed that valor made him worthy of a polite reply.

"Indeed," Rosanna answered evenly, "your father was often a guest here. I was saddened to hear of his recent death. You have my sympathy."

Chandler's lips twisted into a cynical smile. "Pray save your sympathy for someone else. My father wouldn't have grieved for my death. Why should I for his?"

The words sounded harsh, but Rosanna saw the hurt dulling Chandler's blue eyes and was moved. For the briefest moment, she was tempted to let him know she well understood his pain, but the rigid pride of his manner told her that such familiarity would be most unwelcome. She resumed the conversation smoothly, as if she'd seen nothing. "Lord Leighton, I must apologize for mistaking your identity. A problem with Giles's family has been vexing me and I—well I certainly shouldn't be jabbering on about it to some stranger. I shall handle it." Her voice sharpened. "That aside, I still don't see—"

"Please, milady," he interrupted, the roguish swagger back in his smile, "might we sit down? It is cursed difficult to remain at daggers' points while pacing about the room. Destroys the concentration for battle, you know."

Before Rosanna could protest, he took her arm, sat her down on the settee, and ensconced himself on a neighboring cushion. She glanced at him. "Are we to do battle, sir? I hope not. I fear I would be bested quite easily."

His eyes darkened as his glance slowly caressed her face. "I wonder," he murmured with seductive warmth. "You appear not to be the usual goose-witted female. Battle with you might indeed be diverting."

"Not goose-witted? You do turn such a pretty compliment, sir," she mocked, not at all liking the unwanted flutter his look and words caused in her heart. A rake's glibness, nothing more, she reminded herself sternly. Yet a warm blush slid up her cheeks. "We have wandered far from the point, my lord," she insisted firmly. "May I suggest that, before I set up a well-bred screech, you explain this nonsense about being my guardian?"

"Unfortunately, milady, it is not nonsense. I only wish it were. I won't hesitate to admit this . . . new responsibility . . . came as much of a surprise to me as it does to you. It quite knocked me off my pins. It seems our fathers made an agreement ages ago to tend each other's families if one died before his children had reached their majority. They might have been in their cups when they did it, although it's hard to imagine my father ever touching the devil's brew, as he called it. In any case, they left two hand-written wills. Crumbee, my solicitor, found the blasted documents amidst my father's papers while he was settling the estate. Here"—he handed her the single sheet of vellum—"I brought it with me."

Rosanna read the brief document. There was no denying her father's bold handwriting, or his meaning, she admitted, a frown of displeasure creasing her forehead. The guardianship was stated most clearly. How very vexing! After her experience with Giles, she wanted no man interfering in her life. "Surely it's not legal if it wasn't properly witnessed," she protested.

"I suggested that to old Crumbee myself, but to no avail. A will's a will and that's that, he maintained. Believe me, becoming a guardian is dashed inconvenient for me as well!"

No doubt, she fumed silently, flicking a look at him through lowered lashes. If only half the *on dits* about him were true, he must find it monstrously inconvenient to have such a business intrude upon his pleasures. Then, before she could stifle the thought, her heart conceded that the rumors must be true; this man would be the devil to resist if he chose to dance attendance.

Her breath quickened at the idea. The intensity of the emotion jolted her, but displeasure followed quickly. She'd experienced something like this feeling before with Giles, and look what folly that had led to! For her own peace of mind, she'd best put a quick end to this stuff-and-nonsense so that he wouldn't tarry!

"It's absurd, my lord!" she insisted, her voice betraying no hint of the tumult his presence triggered within her. "I can see where your father might claim authority; but you, my lord, are obviulsy not the man my father intended to care for his family. That alone will overset the matter."

"Unfortunately, it does not. The will mentions only that the Earl of Leighton is to be guardian. It does not specify which earl. I assumed that title when my father died. According to Crumbee, there is nothing you or I can do. The law is quite precise on this point."

"I am twenty-four, Lord Leighton. I certainly don't need a guardian."

"That's very clear, it's true."

"How ungallant! Do you always cast a woman's age back at her? I must say that is a devilish bad habit!"

"Don't fly up in the boughs. I've been accused of having many bad habits where women are concerned, but dealing out insults isn't one of them. I've found flattery to be much more profitable. I meant only that you appear to have more sense than the usual schoolroom miss. It may mean that we shall deal together better than I expected."

A smile of remembered conquests softened the firm lines of his mouth. "I don't share your confidence, sir," Rosanna replied stiffly, disliking the thought of all those other women he'd held in his arms. "I have been my own mistress for a goodly spell and have managed this estate without a man's guiding hand. Breaking easily to a bridle is something I won't do. I don't want or need a guardian meddling in my affairs. That would be most troublesome!" She gave a stubborn toss of her dark curls.

"We have no quarrel on that issue, milady." Chandler nodded, then leaned back casually against the arm of the sofa. "It's far from my intention to meddle in your affairs. It's your sisters—twins, I believe—who drag us into this damnable coil. They're not of age. Since by your father's will I am legally responsible for them, there is nothing we can do."

"Nonsense! Lucinda and Cecily aren't even kindred

of yours. They may not be of legal age, but I am. It makes not a particle of sense that I shouldn't continue as their guardian. This scrap of paper"—she insisted, thrusting the will back at him—"should alter nothing."

"I'm afraid it's our bad luck that it does. Old Crumbee explained it quite plainly. According to English law, if a man is named as guardian, the responsibility can not be shrugged aside or given to another. Not even to a sister."

"This is preposterous!" Rosanna snapped, her cheeks growing warm. "I shall speak bluntly, sir. We may be provincial here in Somerset, but we do receive the *Gazette*. It's no secret that you're linked prominently with the Regent's fast set. Furthermore, ah"—a blush crept up her cheeks, but she didn't stop—"there have been other rumors attached to your name. I hardly believe you would be the proper guardian for my sisters!"

Chandler's blue eyes flashed like the hardest sapphires. "You offered brandy earlier. Now I accept," he growled, getting to his feet and stomping across the room to a sideboard on which the decanter stood. "Fencing with you gives me a thirst!"

Rosanna watched him angrily splash some of the amber liquid in a crystal snifter. No doubt he was furious she'd thrown his amorous adventures up to him, but she didn't care. Lucinda and Cecily had to be protected.

The well-aged brandy must have soothed some of his irritation, because his frown was gone when he looked back across the study at her. Their gazes locked. Rosanna refused to lower her eyes. She didn't doubt for an instant that his quizzing usually put women aflutter, but she was determined not to be added to that long list.

Chandler took another sip of brandy and smiled one of his most engaging smiles, which she'd heard were famed for their ability to melt even the haughtiest matrons. "Lady Wythe, pardon my foul temper. I am acting the dolt." He shook his head as if disturbed by her ability to trigger his usually controlled temper. "Somehow we seem destined to draw sparks. But no matter. I assure you we're getting in a spin over nothing. I fancy that if we put our heads together, we can brush through this mess quite handsomely. The last thing I want is to be responsible for a couple of schoolroom misses. Let me pour you a glass of ratafia, and we can conspire."

He resumed his seat beside her and handed her the cordial. Tapping her glass with his, he toasted, "To circumvention."

"Sir?" Rosanna asked, puzzled. "Pray, what do you mean?"

"I mean we're going to abide by the letter of the law, but not the spirit." He downed the remainder of his brandy. "Lady Wythe, rest assured I don't care a jot about this damned guardianship. You appear up to snuff. As far as I can judge, you've been handling the estate admirably. I see no need for me to interfere." He raised a rakish eyebrow. "London has its attractions for me, and frankly I don't care to waste time rusticating in Somerset!"

"I'm quite sure you have—how shall I phrase this?— many other interests to fill your hours," Rosanna replied tartly. "I'm delighted that Lucinda, Cecily, and I won't be a bother to you."

"What a little hellcat you are, dear lady," he murmured in a velvety tone. "Any more words like those, and I may decide to take this guardianship business seriously." Very slowly, very deliberately, Chandler slid nearer to her. His eyes darkened with a fiery glow that made Rosanna's blood race. She tried to rise, but his arm barred her way.

"It's obvious that someone needs to curb your impertinent tongue," he observed, cupping her chin with a strong hand. "You tempt me to have a go at it. I have always found good sport in taming a spirited filly."

The warmth of his caress sent disturbing shivers down Rosanna's spine. She didn't like the way his slightest touch and the warmth of his gaze could ruffle her composure. With a tug, she pulled her head away. "Please have done, sir! I'm not one of your London flirts!"

His deep laugh echoed through the room. "You have no fear on that score, milady. In my experience with the petticoat line, I have found few women as spirited as you. I admit that does give you a certain appeal. Furthermore," he added, allowing his eyes to rake lingeringly over her figure, "you'd be a cozy armful for some man, but my weakness for blondes is well known. You may rest easy."

"Then I shall be forever grateful I'm not fair-haired, for I've had my fill of rakes," Rosanna countered sharply, twisting her wedding ring.

They stared at each other for long moments, their eyes doing silent battle. Chandler was first to look away. His jaw clenched, and when he turned back to face her, she was surprised to see him hold out his hand. "May I suggest a truce, Lady Wythe? Facing Napoleon's cannons was easier than dueling with you. Besides, we're making cakes of ourselves over nothing."

Rosanna put her hand hesitantly in his. She looked down at the entwined clasp and swallowed nervously. His touch moved her far more than she cared to admit. She enjoyed the warm grasp for brief moments before pulling away. Folding her hands primly in her lap, she acknowledged, "Indeed, it is a lowering thought, Lord Leighton, but I'm forced to agree with you. I think things should pass off relatively well if we do not let our tempers explode again."

"I agree completely." He smiled.

Rosanna studied him. He might be a rake, but there was no denying that his smile was devilishly appealing. No doubt it was a great asset in his amorous capers! She reassured herself how vastly lucky she was to be immune to its pull. Yet an answering smile came readily to her lips.

"Shall we proceed with our conspiring, my lord? As I recall, before our unfortunate set-to, you were assuring me that you had no intention of meddling in my affairs. I thank you for that. There is one other favor I wish to ask. My sisters are away from the house just now. Tuesday is their day at the vicarage. Mrs. Bromley is trying to teach them tatting." Her dimples deepened as she admitted, "It's a hopeless endeavor, I fear. We Millbourne woman have never been known for our domestic skills. If you can spare the time, I would like you to stay until they return so that I may make you acquainted with them. They should be back within the hour."

"Certainly. Even so lax a guardian as I intend to be should have at least a nodding acquaintance with his wards."

Rosanna's first reaction was pleasure that the matter had been settled between them with such ease; then, uncomfortably, she realized that she would have to fill another hour. That thought threw her into the fidgets. What was she going to do with him? If they sat chatting, there was sure to be another dust-up, for guarding her tongue had never been one of her virtues. The silence stretched. She cast about nervously in her mind for an idea. Ah, it was simple. Her custom was to ride each morning before breakfast. This week, though, was the end of the quarter, and checking the baliff's books had replaced her usual gallop. She turned to Chandler.

"May I suggest a ride across our lands while we wait?" she suggested formally. "The view from the high meadow is quite lovely at this time of year."

"A very pleasing idea, Lady Wythe. My primary seat is in Kent, and Somerset is unknown to me. I will enjoy comparing farming practices. You see," he observed with a roguish grin as they both rose from the settee, "not all my 'interests' are in London."

"I stand corrected." She dropped a curtsy. "Please help yourself to another glass of brandy. It will take me only a few moments to change."

Rosanna instructed Hobart to tell the groom to saddle Firefly, then hurried up the curving staircase to her bed chamber. Without conscious thought, she reached for her new riding habit, in richest bottle-green, which the village seamstress had delivered recently. The silky velvet flowed under her fingertips as she lifted the garment from the armoire. Holding it up in front of her, she pivoted to face the cheval glass. A warm smile lighted her face as she saw how the deep color made her eyes sparkle. Then her smile faded, replaced by a disapproving frown.

What a ninnyhammered impulse! For a moment she'd felt an urge to see if she could spark some interest in the rakish Lord Leighton. Had she run mad? What a doltish idea! Why should she care what he thought of her? Her chin tilted stubbornly. Did she want to be like all the other silly chits who preened for him? That would only feed the high opinion he already held of himself. Instead, she pulled her usual habit from the armoire, laid it on the bed, and began unlacing her bodice.

Besides, she decided firmly, letting her black bombazine dress fall to the floor, she was well past preening for any man. A much younger Rosanna had spent hours standing for fittings and enduring having her hair cut and crimped into the latest mode, trying desperately to please Giles. And it had been for nothing. For all he cared, she could have been a female mushroom. His notice, his desire, was elsewhere, she recalled painfully, seeing again in her mind's eye the entwining of naked legs and arms the afternoon she had walked unexpectedly into the barn and found Giles making love in the hay to one of his light-skirts.

She angrily shrugged away the remembrance and yanked on her old habit, which felt comfortably familiar sliding over her slender body. She would dress only to please herself. Anyone else, Lord Leighton included, could go to the devil! She took one swipe at her long hair with the brush, pulled it back with a black ribbon, and started downstairs.

When Rosanna walked back through the doorway, Chandler glanced up, looking surprised. She had changed so quickly, his brandy was only half-drunk. Seeing him run an experienced eye over the well-worn habit and her carelessly arranged hair, she lifted her chin defiantly. At least he wouldn't think she was dangling any lures for him. It would do him good to learn there was at least one woman not scheming to become Countess Leighton!

Chandler tossed off the rest of his drink, rose, and offered his arm to escort her outside. A look of surprise flashed across his face again when the groom led out Rosanna's horse. Instead of the usual docile prodders most of the *tonnish* ladies favored, she intended to mount a prancing stallion.

"Have no fear, my lord," she said with amusement, noting his wary expression. "I can handle Firefly. Riding is my one accomplishment."

"What? Your only one? Do you mean you don't paint insipid watercolors, warble off-tune, or pluck at some infernal harp?" He wiped his brow dramatically with an imaginary handkerchief. "A vast relief, to be sure! Off you go, man." He dismissed the hovering groom. "I claim the honor of helping your mistress mount."

Making a step with his locked hands, he threw Rosanna into the saddle. "Perhaps you do need a guardian after all, milady. Your grooms have become careless." He ran his hand over the horse's side. "This cinch is quite frayed. Better have it replaced, or one day you and your saddle will part company from your horse rather uncomfortably."

"I shall tend to it, sir. Meet you at the woods."

A confident smile touched her lips as her gentle tap to Firefly's flanks sent him off at a bruising gallop. She spared a quick glance back at Chandler and saw him swing into the saddle and charge after her. His horse was no doubt the one that had seen him through several campaigns on the Continent, but even its powerful strides couldn't easily match those of her horse.

The grounds in front of Millbourne Hall were well tended. No gullies or hummocks slowed their chase.

The wind whipping through Rosanna's hair loosened it from the black ribbon and it tumbled wildly about her. The sound of thundering hooves told her Lord Leighton was closing and at the meadow's end they were neck-and-neck. Reining in her horse sharply, Rosanna slowed Firefly to a walk as Chandler halted his own mount. She could feel a healthy flush on her face and knew her eyes were shining when she turned toward him. When they had started the ride, the air between them had been tinged a bit with reserve. Words spoken in irritation, his presumptions, and her failure to curb her tart tongue, had made for cool feelings. But their mad gallop had produced a thaw.

With genuine pleasure Rosanna exclaimed, "That was marvelous! I vow it has been a vast age since I've had a dash like that." She regarded his black stallion with a practiced eye. "You ride a prime piece of blood cattle, my lord. My compliments."

"It's gratifying to know that there is at least one thing about me of which you approve," he jested.

"I always approve of a man who knows his horseflesh. Did you find him at Tattersall's? I long to go there." Rosanna sighed and reached down to pat the powerfully arched neck of her horse. "But London seems a long way away."

"No, I didn't find Bucephalus at Tattersall's. You might say we are two of a kind. As I recall, you wanted me to go to the devil. Well, Bucephalus almost beat me there."

Rosanna tilted her head to one side and smiled so that the sunlight played over her dimples. "Yes, I can see the resemblance. You both have a touch of Lucifer about you, especially around the eyes. A rakish gleam, I believe it's called."

"Touché!" Chandler laughed.

Rosanna inclined her head an inch to accept his compliment. "Now tell me how Bucephalus almost became acquainted with the devil." Her gaze ran appreciatively over his magnificent lines. "I can see why Lord Satan coveted such a horse. It's wonderful you saved him."

"Indeed, he is an excellent piece of horseflesh now. I had a hell of a time with him along the way, though."

"Oh? I find it difficult to imagine that anyone could give you a hard time, my lord."

"Do you? Then you must have conveniently forgotten

this afternoon," he countered, his blue eyes alight with humor. "Do you wish to hear of Bucephalus's rescue or shall we resume our duel to freshen your memory?"

"The tale of Bucephalus, please. My sword arm is getting weary."

"Not likely!" He laughed again. "We could have used the likes of you at Talavera, when we were trying to rout the French. In any case, I met my equine friend here while on leave. A group of us decided to take in the races at Newmarket. Early one morning we heard a fracas erupting in a far paddock. Men were shouting and tearing about with uncoiled ropes. In the middle, rearing and pawing the air, was Bucephalus."

A cold anger chilled his eyes to an icy sapphire blue as he remembered. "His owner had tried to break him using sharpened spurs. By the time I got there, blood was dripping from a dozen wounds on his flanks." He glanced back now at the horse's flanks. "The scars are still there."

"How cruel!" Rosanna cried, tears clouding her eyes. "How could anyone do that to an animal? The owner should have been shot!"

Chandler chuckled at the vehemence in her tone. "I couldn't agree with you more. But that day, Bucephalus was almost shot, not the owner. I don't suppose I have to tell you that my friend here took strong exception to such ill-use. In fact, he almost killed the man."

"He would have deserved it!"

"No doubt. But the owner saw differently. It took a fat purse to keep the bullet from between Bucephalus's eyes."

"Thank heavens you were there."

"Yes, I count myself lucky now. However, there was a time when I was trying to put a saddle on his back that

I almost wished I'd forgotten all about those blasted races."

"What else did you expect, my lord? When two odiously stubborn beings meet, it's bound to be a monumental struggle," Rosanna teased pertly.

"Worthy opponents, milady!" He leaned forward and scratched the horse between his ears. "Eventually, Bucephalus and I came to an understanding." He met her gaze, a lazy smile on his mouth. "It was a battle I enjoyed winning. There isn't a creature on God's earth I can't break . . . given enough time."

Rosanna's face grew hot. She well realized he wasn't referring merely to horses. How many women had he broken as well? A dozen, a score, or had he lost count? She didn't intend to join the list. She returned his smile calmly. "Bucephalus aside, then I can conclude that you've only met poor spirited creatures!"

"Perhaps. Or perhaps my luck is only now changing."

CHAPTER
Two

As they entered the woods, Rosanna commented, "Thank you for accompanying me, my lord. It's a pleasure to ride with someone again. After your long journey out here, I wouldn't have blamed you, had you wished to remain in Millbourne Hall and commune with that brandy decanter. It was riding hell-for-leather, I believe you said." She smiled.

Chandler's eyes darkened. "As I said before, such cant phrases are unbecoming to a lady."

"That is true, sir. I shall endeavor to remain missish whenever you are about. Is this more proper?" she asked, pursing her lips primly.

"Indeed it is—it's properly boring!" he laughed. "Come, milady, let's have done with this fencing. Tell me what your sisters are like. Do they ride like you do?"

"No, I fear they can't claim even that accomplishment. Don't misunderstand, my lord," she added quickly. "They're delightful girls—well-mannered, sweet, unassuming. Everything one could wish for. I'm sure you'll like them."

"Perhaps. Although," he admitted, tossing her a quick glance, "unassuming misses have never been to my taste. I've always enjoyed the more spirited types."

"Spirited blondes, as I recall," Rosanna challenged.

"That's true. At least until recently."

21

Before she could reply, he said, "Tell me about your lands. Do you farm, or is this sheep country?"

Their slow walk along the wooded path was more pleasurable than Rosanna would have thought possible. She enjoyed the chance to talk with a man, as she had with her father. Lucinda and Cecily were good companions in many ways, but they paid scant attention to managing the estate. As Rosanna conversed with Chandler about fertilizer, enclosure practices, and crop rotation, she was forced to admit that he had not lied. He did have other interests besides the string of *tonnish* ladies the *Gazette* coupled with his name.

She felt wistful as they emerged from the woods into the shimmering sunlight of the high meadow. She watched him riding so tall, so strong, beside her, and her throat tightened. She almost wished Chandler hadn't shared this serious side of his nature with her. It made him less the rake and thus vastly more unsettling for her peace of heart. Well, she thought with a sigh, he would leave soon enough.

Spurring her horse forward, Rosanna rode up to a small knoll and stopped. With a sweep of her hand, she gestured to the scene. "This is what I wanted to show you."

As he looked down upon her home, a contented smile softened her mouth when she saw the appreciative gleam in his eye. She was proud of Millbourne, of its unique twisting chimneys and diamond-paned windows that bespoke its Elizabethan origins, of the mellow pink brick that tied the rather haphazard later additions together into a harmonious whole. It pleased her that Chandler liked it also.

While he continued to inspect her sprawling property, Rosanna inspected him. The word "magnificent" leaped to her mind again. She couldn't keep her eyes from wandering over the expanse of his powerful shoulders or the curve of his thighs where his hard muscles strained the seams of his riding breeches. Here, out in the open, he looked totally at ease and in command.

In command... The thought snared a memory. Lord Leighton most assuredly was that, she admitted to herself. In fact, if she recalled the tale correctly, as it had been so luridly reported in the *Gazette,* his determination to be in command had landed him before a court-martial tribunal. The details returned to her. In the heat of the battle at Talavera, he had countermanded a direct order from Wellington. Only the Iron Duke's bellowing insistence that his daring tactic, whether ordered or not, had turned the tide, saved him from being cashiered.

Seeing him now astride Bucephalus, Rosanna had to acknowledge that he easily looked the hero. Man and horse were indeed two of a kind, as he's said. Both were powerful, dominating, and... incredibly masculine. Blast it all, she raged. Why had she suggested they ride? He had seemed far safer in the study!

The clatter of an approaching rider snapped her attention away from her disquieting thoughts. When she glanced up and guessed who was coming, her lips tightened with strain and a muffled oath escaped her lips.

Chandler glanced at her, then across the high meadow to the approaching rider.

"I believe the cousin approaches, milady," he observed. He began to move to draw his horse protectively in front of her, but the militant set to her chin must have convinced him to stay back.

"I fear that is the case," she muttered.

"The rumormongers' tales were indeed correct. The chap is a dandy or worse. I've seen him hanging about the fringes of the *ton*. Hardly top of the trees, though, and no wonder! Such abominable taste. Even from this distance his puce waistcoat offends my sensibilities," Chandler commented.

Sighting them, the man urged his nag into a trot. The numerous fobs hanging from the chain stretched across his ample stomach jiggled as he bounced up and down in the saddle. "No bottom. Cow-handed as well," Chandler whispered. "Perhaps you should offer to give him riding lessons."

Rosanna knew he was trying to draw a smile from her with his jests, but it didn't work. "I would sooner cross swords with a pirate!" she vowed. Her hands tightened on the reins, causing Firefly to shy nervously.

At least the man coming toward them looked as displeased as she felt, which made her feel a bit better. No doubt he was wishing Giles had been thoughtful enough not to cash in his chips so the Millbourne fortune would have stayed in the Wythe coffers and he wouldn't have to come wooing. Or perhaps it was Lord Leighton, towering at her side, that inspired his glower. Rosanna glanced at the man beside her. For the first time, she was glad her father had written that will.

The dandy reined his hack before Rosanna, ignoring the earl's presence. "Ah, my dear cousin," he effused, bowing in his saddle as low as his corpulent figure would allow. "I beg you grant me the right to call you such. Giles was ever so dear to me. I know you feel his loss as keenly as I."

When Rosanna remained rigidly silent, he continued, "He spoke to me often of your beauty, but his description pales in your presence." Sweeping his hand before him, he vowed, "The bluebells and daffodils of this meadow ought to hang their heads in shame when you ride by. Your countenance puts them to the blush."

She saw him cast a quick look to see how his compliments were sitting. When it was obvious that his flattery was failing to melt the hard glitter in her eyes, he apparently decided to change tactics. "How rude of me to patter on when formal introductions are lacking. Since we're kindred, let us not be skittish over formalities. My name is Wilbert." He bowed again. "Might I have the honor of addressing you as Rosanna?"

"No, you may *not* address me as such!" Rosanna snapped. "I have no desire to recognize any more of Giles's family than is necessary. I bow to Lord Wythe in the parish church. That is sufficient."

"Ah, milady, how can you be so cruel? You know the Wythe family holds you close to their hearts."

"What they wish to hold close is my purse. That shall not be!"

Refusing to take her meaning, Sir Wilbert clapped his hand over his heart and rushed on. "I can see you are rightly miffed because I failed to speed to you with my condolences the moment dear Giles's death became known. It is your right to be most angry with me," he moaned forlornly. "Know that only the press of my affairs in London kept me from your side. I beg forgiveness."

"You have a most convenient hearing, sir," Rosanna retorted. "I don't care a fig that you failed to call. In fact—"

"You are indeed an angel of understanding," he interrupted. "I'm delighted I have not sunk totally beneath your reproach. It gladdens my heart."

Rosanna's exasperated sigh drew a look of concern from Chandler. His tone bristled with authority as he insisted, "Sir, you have heard Lady Wythe. She does not wish to recognize you." When Sir Wilbert tried to retort,

Chandler commanded, "That is enough! Let's hear no more. I'm sure Lady Wythe is as tired as I am of your gibberish. If you continue to press this relationship, I shall advise her to attach your cousin's estate. It is my understanding that she disavowed all claim at the time of her husband's death. She still has time to reassert her claim." His voice grew harsh. "As heir to what little is left, you'd best heed my words!"

Turning in his saddle, Chandler gave Rosanna a conspiratorial wink. "Milady, Crumbee, my solicitor, stands ready to be of service to you."

Her eyes brimming with laughter, she returned his smile. What a delightful tactic he'd popped up with. "It *is* a thought," she acknowledged, nodding thoughtfully. "Thank you for the suggestion, Lord Leighton." Erasing all mirth from her face, she returned to the frowning Wilbert. "I shall consider precisely that, should it become necessary."

Ignoring her, Sir Wilbert struck out at Chandler. "Hartwick," he snarled, "you can bloody well keep your suggestions to yourself. This is none of your affair!"

"There you're wrong." Chandler's words were as stern as Sir Wilbert's were angry. "Lord Millbourne left his daughters under my protection. I intend to be a very watchful guardian, both here and in London."

"Guardian? Gammon!" he raged. "Millbourne's been dead a long spell. Why should you show up only now? A Banbury tale, that's what it is!"

"I tell no tales, as well you know." Chandler regarded Rosanna with deviltry in his eyes. "Explain to this most encroaching fellow that you are indeed under my protection. Perhaps he will believe you."

Her eyes narrowed. Chandler's amusement was evident, as was his intent. He was delighting in forcing her to admit to his guardianship. She almost spoke words to deny his claim, but stopped herself. Could she really bear another go-round with Giles's family? More than anything, she wanted to be rid of them! She flung a frustrated glance of defeat at Chandler, then admitted, "Lord Leighton speaks the truth. Father's will only recently came to light." She swallowed. "His lordship is indeed our legal guardian."

"How convenient to have a cozy widow under your protection, milord," Sir Wilbert sneered in a nasty voice. "It saves the expense of some light-skirt."

Chandler's fist closed angrily around his riding crop and he raised it threateningly. "If you don't want those foul words shoved back down your filthy gullet, you'd best leave!"

"You've not heard the last of this business," Wilbert warned before wheeling his horse sharply and bouncing off.

Chandler glanced at Rosanna, a concerned expression on his face. She knew he expected her to be horribly embarrassed by Sir Wilbert's slur against her name, but instead she was having a difficult time stifling giggles. "What a ridiculous figure Sir Wilbert cut!" she cried. "And you, sir, aside from that unkind thrust to make me avow your guardianship, were the most complete hand. Pray, how did you know I wanted no money from Giles's family?

"Lady Wythe, you're really not to be beat on any suit," Chandler avowed, an eyebrow raising in surprise. "I expected no less than a fit of the vapors." A hint of respect registered in his gaze. "But to answer your question, when you're leading a regiment into battle, you'd best learn to judge people quickly and correctly, or the River Styx will be your next stop. That's how I guessed you took nothing but your freedom from your husband's estate."

Rosanna's dimples deepened. "How distressing this must be for you. You thought yourself well rid of us. Now you've had to extend your protection all the way to London. A most vexing situation, I'm sure!"

"Can you doubt it?" He grinned back. "Nevertheless, I shall endeavor to endure."

Sighing dramatically, Rosanna fluttered her eyelashes. "I vow, sir, I'm quite overcome with your bravery!"

"And I vow," he countered with a roguish smile, "that someday I shall curb that capricious tongue of yours."

Rosanna became more serious. "Indeed, Lord Leighton, I wish to thank you. I could have managed Giles's cousin alone, but the scene would have been vastly unpleasant."

"I'm convinced you could have, as well," he complimented her. "Any woman who can control a great whacking beast like the horse you ride should be able to set down an encroaching toad like that Wilbert fellow. Nonetheless, I'm glad I could be of some small service. My warning will give him pause for a spell, I'm sure." His smile broadened. "No man with the abominable taste to sport a puce waistcoat could possibly possess an ounce of courage or persistence."

"Quite true! After seeing his odious preference in attire, I'm doubly sorry for calling you a dandy."

"As well you should be, milady! A grievous insult, indeed. My tailor and valet may never recover."

"And you, sir? Are you not insulted?"

"Parading about like a peacock on the strut may be well and good for those who lack anything else to recommend them. I should prefer to be remembered for other things."

Rosanna almost retorted that rumor of those "other

things" had penetrated even into backwater Somerset, but she recalled the words. Give the man his due, she decided. His reckless heroics in the Peninsula were equally well known. Perhaps those were what he wished remembered.

Chandler glanced up at the sun. "I judge the hour near spent. Shall we return?"

They talked of commonplace topics until they broke from the woods. Rosanna was about to challenge him to another gallop when she looked toward Millbourne Hall and saw a tall, dark-haired man waving a hand at her in greeting. "It's Adrian!" she cried. Without a backward glance at Chandler, she spurred her mount into a gallop.

"How is Ginger?" Rosanna asked as Adrian swung her out of the saddle. "Has she foaled yet?"

"Indeed she has." Adrian smiled, his hands spanning her waist. "That's why I came. Knew you would want the news the instant the colt dropped. Birthed a sweet-goer, she did. Give him three years and I'll lay a monkey he'll best Firefly here," he joked, stroking the stallion's proud neck.

"It's a bet!" Rosanna saw Adrian's black eyes dart toward Chandler, who'd dismounted and was walking toward them. His hands fell from her waist as she exclaimed, "Where have my manners flown to, chattering on like this when you two gentlemen haven't been introduced? Adrian, Viscount Cameron, become acquainted with Chandler Hartwick, Earl Leighton." Turning to Chandler, she explained, "The viscount's land marches with ours to the north."

Chandler's words were polite as he and Adrian exchanged greetings, but Rosanna detected an unexplained edge of roughness in his voice. Reflecting back on the past few moments, she also remembered the flash of blue ice that had shot through his gaze when he'd seen Adrian's hands lifting her from Firefly's back. A delicious idea occurred to her. Was he beginning to feel merely a bit proprietary because of this responsibility as her guardian, or was there the slightest chance he'd felt a spark of jealousy? But the most unsettling thought was wondering why she cared.

These muddled musings were interrupted by the sound of a pony cart crunching down the drive. Rosanna turned to greet her sisters, but only Lucinda and her abigail were in the cart. It tugged at Rosanna's heart just a tiny bit to see how Chandler's eyes widened in surprise as her sister neared. In truth, she couldn't blame him, because even she had to admit that Lucinda was nothing less than a vision, with guinea-gold curls bobbing above eyes as blue as cornflowers and a face that cast the local belles into the shade.

"Smashing, simply smashing!" Chandler uttered, obviously finding it difficult to draw his gaze away from Lucinda's fair countenance.

Rosanna felt a second sad tug at her heart. It wasn't envy, for she loved her sisters far too well to begrudge them their beauty. Still, she couldn't help wishing some man would look at her with such admiration.

Shrugging such hen-witted notions aside, she moved to his lordship's side and agreed, "Indeed she is smashing, and her sister is an identical copy. Pray, don't make the obvious comparison with me. I've learned to accept my looks. I favor my father's side of the family, more's the pity."

Unable to watch Chandler struggling to think of something gallant to say to her, she turned and walked off to greet her sister. "Where is Cecily?" she asked. "She wasn't taken ill, I hope."

Lucinda shared a warm smile with Adrian, then allowed him to hand her out of the cart before she answered. "Cecily, ill? Hardly! Vicar Bromley's son is down from Oxford." Rolling her eyes heavenward, she explained, "You can guess what that meant. Cecily decided to stay and practice. She wanted to see how long it would take before she could make him stutter."

"Lucinda! That is quite enough!"

"It's true, Rosanna. You know what a flirt she is, and—Oh, very well, I shall be silent." Lucinda stopped when her older sister frowned warningly. "Vicar Bromley said he'd see her home after tea."

"At least you're here. Come, I want you to meet Lord Leighton, your new guardian."

"Lord Lei . . . Oh, Rosanna, I am sorry. I didn't realize we had a guest," she apologized, a delicate blush tinting her cheeks as she glanced hesitantly at Lord Leighton.

Lucinda made a graceful curtsy to Chandler after introductions were made. There was no flutter of eyelashes, no coquettish smile, no attempt to engage his attention. Rosanna smiled with pride when her sister's manner, as promised, was unaffectedly correct to the shade. As she had reflected many times before, she wondered how many *tonnish* ladies would be so innocent of vanity if they possessed her sister's beauty.

When Adrian heard the word "guardian," he interrupted their exchange of greetings. "Wards . . . guardian . . . what is this nonsense?"

Knowing instinctively that women usually exerted every wile to attract Chandler's attention, Rosanna assumed a contrary role. She was rewarded by seeing a surge of anger darken his eyes as she laid her fingers possessively on Adrian's arm. "Come, join us for luncheon," she urged the viscount. "I'll tell you everything then." She went a dozen paces before she pretended to recall the presence of the other man. "Oh, Lord Leighton, please join us as well." Casually assuming he would follow, she and Adrian continued toward the great arched door leading into Millbourne Hall.

"Was your tatting lesson successful?" Rosanna heard Chandler ask Lucinda in a bored drawl, and Rosanna breathed a sigh of relief. Her tactic was working so far.

Once in the house, Rosanna directed, "Lucinda, please sit to Lord Leighton's left so you two might become acquainted."

Throughout the meal she observed Chandler trying to make polite chitchat with her sister. Obviously, holding a conversation with a miss just out of the schoolroom wasn't his idea of an enjoyable way to wile away an afternoon. He made no secret of his boredom, barely stifling his yawns. It pleased her to see that he wasn't trying to set up a flirtation with Lucinda. Finally Rosanna took pity on him and asked him about his experiences with Wellington, which allowed Chandler to turn his attention from his newfound ward.

When the hour came for Chandler to take his leave, Rosanna accompanied him to the door while Adrian stayed with Lucinda to organize a game of jackstraws. "Lady Wythe," the earl said when they'd reached the entry hall, "this day has been far more enjoyable than I supposed possible when old Crumbee showed up with that blasted will."

"For me, too," she confessed softly, wishing he wouldn't smile at her in such a devilishly endearing way. "Lord Leighton, I'm not unmindful of the gratitude we owe you. If there is any way I can repay your kindness, please let me know."

His eyes glittered. "There is one way," he murmured,

carrying her hand to his lips. "Must we stand on appearances? My name is Chandler. Might I have the honor you denied that Wilbert chap and call you Rosanna? I vow that if you do, I shall never put you to the blush by wearing a puce waistcoat."

His lingering kiss on her palm sent waves of longing through her. She determined to yank her hand away . . . yet the strength to do so failed to come. As if it had a will of its own, her hand remained nestled snugly in his warm grasp.

His eyes rose to meet hers. "Rosanna is a lovely name. Grant me its use," he urged with velvet persuasion.

A rake's glibness, nothing more, she warned herself again. Still, she couldn't keep her heart from thudding uncomfortably as she agreed, "Formalities are indeed foolish under the circumstances. My father's will decreed we shall have to deal together, if only scantily"—she swallowed, then added—"Chandler."

Rosanna gave a little tug to free her hand, but he refused to relinquish it. Instead his hold tightened until tingles of warmth spread from his grasp up her arm. His smile deepened as if he knew well the effect he was having on her. Brushing the back of her hand again with his lips, he murmured, "Rosanna, I bid you good day."

He hesitated, then, even though he'd avowed he had no wish to be shackled with the responsibility of being a guardian he added, "If the dandified cousin causes you any more grief, please send a message to me. I'll ride out immediately." Only then did he relinquish her hand.

Watching him swing into the saddle and gallop off, Rosanna was aware of an uncomfortable flutter in her stomach. She lingered on the gravel drive until he was out of sight. It was well that he was gone, she told herself. They needed no *tonnish* lord meddling in their affairs!

Yet for all her brave words, the thought of not seeing Chandler again for a long while brought despondency, not relief. Suddenly she wished for nothing more than the solitude of her bedchamber, but Lucinda and Adrian were waiting for her return. Sighing deeply, she walked back into the house.

Later that night the thoughts and feelings Rosanna had been pushing away all afternoon reappeared to plague her. She tossed in her lonely bed restlessly. Sleep refused to come. Finally, in exasperation, she pulled a warm wrapper about her and went to sit by the window. The full moon cast an eerie light over the formal gardens. It made her feel sad.

She could usually keep the tears away, but not now. There, in the garden beneath the rose trellis, she'd first tasted Giles's kisses. At times it seemed like yesterday to her, instead of five years ago. Rosanna's thoughts spun backward.

It was the spring of her eighteenth year. Her parents had promised her a season in London which had to be canceled when typhus carried off her beloved mother. Now a ball for the local gentry marked the end of her family's year of mourning. Rosanna had been talking with Adrian when Giles walked in. She could picture him yet—tall, slender, his black hair curling handsomely over the collar of his regimentals. Later she'd decided men should never be allowed to court women while dressed in uniform. It made them too devilishly attractive. But she was less wise then, and Giles's red uniform only added to his dashing air. Once he'd taken her hand for the quadrille, she never looked at another man.

The touch of the kisses he gave her that night blinded her heart to the whispers flying about his reputation. Her innocence and inexperience were no obstacles to so skilled a lover. He had captured her heart in no time. Rosanna was young and in love, and even her father's reluctance to approve the match mattered little to her. He begged Rosanna to wait, to be presented to the *ton,* to learn something more of life and men before she settled. But his wise words couldn't compete against the pull of her newly awakened love.

Giles's leave was short. In honeyed phrases he begged her to marry him before he had to return to his regiment. His wooing was so intense that she never questioned why he'd singled her out. She knew only that she wanted him desperately. Finally her father gave his consent and they were wed.

Her bliss lasted a scant week. A few tears fell now on Rosanna's velvet wrapper as she bitterly recalled her deepening disillusionment with her husband. His light-skirts, his weakness for drink, his repeated raids on her dowry—it was shattering.

To her relief, Giles's leave was soon spent and he left. Months passed with nary a letter, until word came that he had fallen at Waterloo. Rosanna cried at the news of his death, but was never sure if she cried for him, for herself, for tarnished love, or for her lost innocence. She returned gratefully to the peace of Millbourne Hall and occupied herself in running the estate for her ailing father. She had thought her tears had dried long ago, but now they were back.

Usually Rosanna fought against recalling the past. It hurt to remember. Why was it nagging her now? Dashing away the tears with the back of her hand, she stood up and paced the room. She tried not to admit Chandler was the cause for her sudden disquiet, but it was useless. His image had planted itself firmly in her mind. Chandler, with roguish glints dancing in his blue eyes. Chandler, whose smile made her heart turn over. Chandler, who . . . Oh, blast the man! Why did he have to come and stir up feelings she had thought were dead?

When Giles's true stamp had become obvious she'd denied him her bed. But those first few love-filled nights of passion had done their damage. Try as she would, she couldn't still the waves of longing, of need, that were her sole companions through the nights that followed. After Giles's death, the feelings had faded with time, but now the familiar ache was back, flooding her body with demands she couldn't deny.

Rosanna yanked the belt of her wrapper tighter. One kiss from a rake, and she was acting the hen-witted fool for a second time! Had she learned nothing from her marriage? A rake never reformed, she reminded herself bitterly, especially one who loudly avowed his preference for fair-haired misses. Well, Chandler could keep his blond chits, she decided with an angry toss of her head. As she remembered, Giles's bit of muslin was straw-haired as well. Truly they were two of a kind, and she was well rid of them both.

Stripping off her wrapper, Rosanna climbed into her cold bed. She welcomed the chill linen sheets against her feverish skin. One last remembrance of Chandler winking at her after his set-to with Wilbert tried to sneak into her thoughts. "No! I will not have it!" she muttered aloud, savagely punching the feather pillow. Forcing her mind to go over and over the columns of figures denoting the quarterly rent payments, she finally managed to drop into a troubled sleep.

CHAPTER
Three

THE TWINS WERE still atwitter about their unexpected guardian at breakfast the next morning. Even Lucinda, who was usually solicitously observant, failed to note Rosanna's pale face and the droop to her usually smiling mouth. She half-listened to the twins' chatter, then looked up when Cecily's teacup clattered down into its saucer. "I shall never forgive that doltish Bromley for keeping me from meeting Lord Leighton," Rosanna's sister fussed, with a toss of her golden curls. "It's so very romantic. A handsome guardian come to rescue us from our dreary existence." She glanced at her twin. "He *is* handsome, isn't he? It will ruin everything if he isn't!"

"Then you'd better be ready to be cast into the dismals, for I didn't find him handsome at all," Lucinda insisted. "He was much too formidable to appeal to me. Heavens, he must have topped fifteen stones. I vow he looked like he'd be more at home striding on the deck of a pirate ship than listening to me rattle on about tatting. What did you think, Rosanna? Did you find him handsome?"

The question jolted her older sister unpleasantly. Rosanna choked over a swallow of tea. Lucinda rushed to her side and began patting her vigorously on the back. Rosanna's composure finally returned, but the heightened color remained tinting her face. "Handsome?" she replied casually, as if considering the idea for the first time. "If the gossip is true, many women find him so. I admit there was a certain reckless arrogance in his manner that might appeal to some silly females."

"Really!" Cecily's blue eyes sparkled. "Do you mean our guardian is a rake? How marvelous!"

"Don't be a tiresome child," Rosanna scolded. "Rake, indeed! That's hardly a proper word to touch a young lady's lips. If I hear such nonsense again, I believe I must forbid those dreadful romances you favor reading. Besides, it doesn't matter. By mutual desire, Lord Leighton's guardianship is to be quite informal. I doubt we'll see him again for a vast age."

"Oh, phoo!" Cecily exclaimed. "The only interesting thing to occur in ever so long and I have to miss it. I've never met a rake and—Oh, very well," she conceded when her sister flashed her an admonishing frown. "I'll forget all about him. But if something else exciting doesn't occur soon, I vow I'll go into a decline."

"Before you take to the couch with your vinaigrette, perhaps you should know I've arranged for Madame Josephina to come out today from Salisbury." Rosanna smiled fondly at her two sisters. "You're almost eighteen. Since our period of mourning is over, I'm sure invitations will soon be arriving for the local routs. I thought you might like to have a few new gowns."

"And what about you?" Cecily asked with a pretty pout. "It quite puts me to the blush to have a sister who deliberately continues to play the dowd. Black is most assuredly not your color!" She clapped her hands excitedly. "We'll all get new wardrobes. Then Rosanna can get out of the dowagers' row and whirl about the dance floor with us."

"I'll do no such thing!" Rosanna insisted. "I'm far too old to be courting attention in such an unbecoming manner."

"You act as if you've been on the shelf for years. Dear sister, you're only twenty-four. You could be quite attractive if you'd only dress in the mode and do something with your hair," Cecily persisted. "I wish you'd let me—"

"No!" Rosanna interrupted firmly. "My pleasure will be in watching you two set Somerset in a spin."

"But . . ." Cecily started to argue.

Lucinda, who had always been more sensitive to the hurt Rosanna still felt over her disastrous marriage, smoothly interjected a suggestion to divert her twin's attention. "Wouldn't it be a good idea to ask Adrian to come teach us the new steps before the parties begin?"

"Oh, Rosanna, please, let's do." Cecily winked at her sister. "I know he wouldn't mind coming if Lucinda asked him. Cleona told me there's a new minuet from France. Maybe he'll know it. Do you think he will, Lucinda?"

Rosanna let her sisters chatter on, smiling to herself. She had seen the delicate blush staining Lucinda's cheeks when she'd spoken Adrian's name. The direction of that interest hadn't escaped Rosanna. Adrian hadn't yet come up to scratch, but she felt certain he would. She was pleased for he'd been a close friend for years and would do nicely for Lucinda.

Cecily was another matter! Rosanna feared her flirtatious nature would lead her into trouble. Cecily meant it all in innocence, but someone might take it amiss. Oh, well, that problem could be handled another day.

Rosanna dropped her napkin on the mahogany table. "We'd best get ready. Madame Josephina should arrive at any moment."

They spent the day enjoyably, examining bolts of brocade silk, dimity, and tulle. As usual, Cecily chose a shade of blue for her gowns, leaving Lucinda with the pinks and pastel yellows. When Cecily had been a young girl, she'd decided blue would be her color and Lucinda had agreed. It was their special way of helping people tell them apart. Rosanna smiled with pride as she watched them stand for their fittings. It didn't really matter what color they wore. They were equally lovely.

After supper they settled down to a game of whist with Hobart sitting in for the fourth hand. Unfortunately, Chandler's image tended to intrude when Rosanna ought to be minding her trumps. Watching Lucinda gather in a trick she herself should have won, Rosanna reminded herself that Chandler had probably cast her from his mind the moment he'd left Somerset. No doubt he was at that moment squiring some fair-haired chit at a romp in London. He wasn't worth another thought! With conscious effort, she thrust away his image and concentrated on her cards.

Rosanna was partly correct. Chandler's evening plans did include seeing a blonde, but Rosanna was wrong in thinking he'd forgotten her. On Wednesdays there were the dances at Almack's. Since the matter of Lord Millbourne's will had been settled so quickly, Chandler had decided to pop in and surprise Lady Pondesbury, his latest flirt. The thought of Elvinia's fair charms made him smile as he tied his cravat in the latest version of the waterfall.

Then, unexpectedly, as his valet was helping him ease into his coat, Elvinia's face faded to be replaced by a woman with masses of long, dark hair, not blond curls. Chandler shook his head, perplexed. Rosanna seemed to be haunting his thoughts. Her gray eyes intrigued him.

As his valet applied the final touches to his evening attire, memories of Rosanna's many moods spun through his mind. He recalled her eyes flashing with anger, sparkling with amusement, and darkening with remembered pain. Most disturbing of all, he remembered her gray eyes shining with laughter as Adrian had lifted her from the saddle. A stab of irritation shot through Chandler as he considered how the other man's hands had tarried about her waist.

Hell and damnation, what was the matter with him? Why should he care if some young buck danced attendance on Rosanna? He had no claim on her. No, there was no reason for him to care, he reminded himself. But quite unexpectedly he did care. He deliberately ignored the feeling as he climbed into the carriage that would take him to Almack's and the blond and lovely Elvinia Pondesbury.

Lady Jersey was the receiving patroness that night as Chandler walked into the famed marriage mart. His friendship with Sally went back a long way, and his greeting was affectionate as he bowed gallantly over her gloved hand.

"Ah, I see the *ton*'s favorite guardian has returned from the wilds of Somerset," she observed.

"Guardian? How did you hear of that, milady?"

"Doltish question, Hartwick. There are no secrets during the season, especially not from me. It's common enough gossip. In fact, Lady Pondesbury was just regaling us with the tale of your plight." Her accent on the name was biting. "She finds it quite amusing that you're saddled with some watering pot of a widow and two schoolroom misses."

"Lady Wythe is no watering pot, and—"

"Spare me the scold." Lady Jersey tapped his arm sharply with her fan. "Those were dear Elvinia's words, not mine." She regarded him with affection. "Personally,

I think the responsibility will do you good!" The door opened to admit several more guests. Before turning to greet them, Lady Jersey suggested, "You'd best make haste to the ballroom, my friend. It seems your latest flirt is quite popular this evening. Lord Colville is making sheep's eyes at Elvinia, but from her flutterings I believe she prefers the addresses of Mr. Tweedsmuir. He's rich as Croesus, they say. Best tend to your fences."

Chandler bent low over her hand before taking his leave. Cocking her head to one side, Lady Jersey studied him again. "You don't seem in a fret over Lady Pondesbury's string of admirers. Are you sure of her affection or are you beginning not to care?" As he started to speak, she held up a restraining hand. "No, don't bother to answer. Best think on it, though."

Glancing over her shoulder toward the door, she sighed. "Oh fie, I see Lady Bigge just waltzed in with the gangling daughter of hers in tow. A born antidote if there ever was one. No doubt I can contrive something, but it shall be difficult."

"Do you never tire of matchmaking, milady?" Chandler teased.

"No. It's a vastly entertaining sport!"

"I count myself lucky to have escaped your snares."

"Your day shall come, my friend." Lady Jersey's smile softened. "I've yet to find a match worthy of you, but I shall. Now off with you."

As Chandler walked past the cardroom, one of his oldest friends, Edward Maitland, emerged. His hazel eyes widened with pleasure. "Ho, Hartwick. Didn't expect to see you here tonight."

"Believe me, I've had my fill of rusticating. It's good to be back in London."

"Even rusticating would be more interesting than this

crop. Don't you agree, gentlemen?" a bored voice drawled at their backs.

There was no mistaking the owner of that voice. "Crop? What crop are you jammering about, Brummell?" Edward asked, moving over to let the other man step between them.

The famous arbiter of the *ton* yawned. "What else? The crop of chits being popped off this season." He waved his hand in a lazy sweep across the dance floor. "Dismal, isn't it? A whole season of squiring female mushrooms!" A hint of deviltry sparked his eyes. "Gentlemen, are we to countenance such a boring prospect? I for one, shall not!"

"What do you propose, George?" Chandler inquired. "Change mushrooms into belles? I don't believe even your abilities could turn that trick."

"A sad truth, but I must agree. Once mutton-faced, always mutton-faced. No, what I have in mind is a challenge to be put in the betting book at White's."

"A challenge to do what?" As Edward shook his head, the one stubborn lock of his carroty hair that would never stay properly brushed flopped down over his forehead. In a useless attempt to keep it in place, he pushed it back, then commented, "If you can't turn these chits into Incomparables, no one can. Don't have your touch, you know."

"Use your imagination, Maitland. This crop is hopeless, but there must be other eligibles not present. Bound to be. Cousins, nieces, and the such. The challenge will be to produce the belle of the *ton*. I'll even get the Prince to lay down a monkey to sweeten the pot."

A devilish smile flitted across Chandler's face as he thought of Brummell's wager. If he wanted to he could win the game easily. All he had to do was produce Lucinda and her twin. He had no doubt they would cause a stir even amongst the jaded *ton*. He smiled again. And, like any man, he did so enjoy winning a wager!

Before he could reflect more on the idea, he spotted Elvinia dancing in one of the cotillion sets with the ever-faithful Neville Tweedsmuir. It crossed his mind briefly to wonder at Sally's question. Was he tiring of the widow Pondesbury? No, he decided, letting his eyes rove slowly over her lush figure. How could anyone tire of such beauty? Tweedsmuir swung her in a turn and Chandler caught her eye. Flashing a brilliant smile, she gave a quick flick of her blond curls, beckoning him to join her after the dance. Chandler nodded in return, then turned back to Brummell and Edward.

When the music ended Elvinia sent Tweedsmuir off for an ice and hurried to Chandler's side. Tucking her fingers securely in the crook of his arm, she cooed, "I had not expected to see you here tonight, Hartwick. La, I can well imagine how dismal that widow must have been to send you back so quickly." She let her body brush lightly up against his. "It's a most delightful surprise," she added throatily.

"I'm glad you're pleased. Your warm greeting is vastly more enjoyable than my reception in Somerset."

"Oh?" Elvinia asked, her smile showing how gratified she was that the widow Wythe hadn't thrown herself into Chandler's arms. "How dreary it must have been for you, and such a bother."

"There you are out. Surprisingly, it was little bother at all," he admitted. Rosanna had, indeed, caused no bother, he mused. In fact, if anything, he was somewhat miffed that she'd so calmly dismissed his offers of help and protection.

"Hartwick, I'm afraid you misjudge us females," Elvinia said. "Instead of being over, the bother may be only now beginning! I wouldn't be at all surprised if the widow Wythe shows up on your doorstep with those two tiresome sisters of hers and demands that, as their guardian, you lend your countenance for a presentation."

"A presentation? Hmmm. But I believe you're wrong," he disagreed, remembering Rosanna's bristling independence. "Lady Wythe said nothing of coming to London."

"That won't make a particle of difference. What woman wouldn't wish to hang on your sleeve? Probably the only reason she hasn't thrown herself back on the marriage mart is because she lacked a *tonnish* connection. This guardianship rubbish is the perfect way for her to return to society. I warn you, unless you want the bother and expense of making a presentation, you'd best stop playing the gallant. Let your solicitor handle this matter from now on. He's competent enough."

Her well-breed screech continued, but Chandler wasn't attending. Of course. How simple, he decided. A presentation! Wasn't it a prime duty of any guardian to see his wards safely wed? The idea of bringing the twins to London for the season reminded him of Brummell's wager. As soon as word spread of the bet, the whole *ton* would be sifting through their rural relations in hopes of finding a diamond of the first water. He would produce not only one, but two! What a deuce of a stir that pair would create.

His thoughts drifted to Rosanna. She was a comely enough piece, he admitted with a smile, even if her sisters did cast her in their shade. Born to the quality, too, and her fortune was respectable enough to tempt many men. Surely she wouldn't wish to rusticate forever. It was time she was safely shackled as well. Dash it all, she couldn't

continue alone. She might claim herself up to snuff, but
not with the likes of Wilbert skulking in the woods! She
needed a husband.

He cast idly through a list of eligible suitors. Balfour?
No, he was too old. Hardinge? No, his country seat was
too far north. Stanfordham? No, he had a paunch. The
reasons became more and more vague as he rejected name
after name. At last he gave up. Surely he could find
someone for Lady Wythe. He didn't think to question
why the idea of Rosanna wedded to anyone else was
slightly distasteful to him.

Elvinia let her hand brush suggestively against Chandler's chest as she moved her fingers down to rest on his
arm. "I can tell you are vastly distracted by all this guardianship nonsense. Truly, it isn't your problem. Didn't
you tell me it was your father that doltish Millbourne
intended to be saddled with his brood, not you? It's not
your responsibility. You have satisfied propriety with
your duty call." She batted her long eyelashes at him.
"Why don't you cast it from your mind so that we can
enjoy the buffet?"

Chandler looked down at the woman by his side as if
seeing her for the first time. "You believe that satisfying
propriety is enough?"

"La, what else is there?" she asked a bit impatiently
when he made no move toward the dining room. "No
one in the *ton* can possibly condemn you. Your obligation
is complete. Pray, let us hear no more of it. I'm quite
fatigued with the whole matter."

Once they were seated in the dining room, Elvinia
suggested, "The crocuses are in bloom at Hampton Court.
Couldn't we take a picnic hamper and ride out tomorrow?
There are many delightful glades to explore along the
way." Her voice dropped to a husky purr. "Some, I hear,
are most secluded."

A spark kindled in Chandler's blue eyes. No doubt of it, Lady Pondesbury was a tempting chit. But it was impossible. "This week won't do, I'm afraid. I have a great many plans to make. Perhaps we can ride out later in the Season." His eyes slid down to caress the plunging décolletage of her gown. "It certainly sounds like a pleasurable outing."

She stamped her tiny kid slipper in exasperation. "La, I shall have to ask Neville to take me then."

Elvinia's increasing possessiveness hadn't escaped Chandler's notice and he had no intention of dancing to her or any other woman's tune. With a casual smile, he agreed. "A smashing idea! I shouldn't want you to miss a treat simply because I'm unavailable. I hear Tweedsmuir is quite the horticulturist. No doubt he can tell you the Latin names of every flower out there. I daresay the outing will be most educational."

When Elvinia pouted and began to beg again, he pulled his arm away from her clutching fingers. "No," he repeated, "I'm busy this week. Being a guardian takes time. As I told you, I have many plans to make."

Late the next afternoon, an elegant traveling coach accompanied by two outriders turned into the drive at Millbourne Hall. The three sisters, who were just leaving to take tea at the vicarage, stopped to watch as the emblazoned door of the carriage swung open and a portly gentleman stepped out.

After making a proper bow, he said to Rosanna, "Lord Leighton sends his compliments, Lady Wythe, and requests you spare me a few moments of your time. I beg leave to present myself." When she nodded he continued, "I am Thaddeus Crumbee, his lordship's solicitor."

Rosanna's eyes darkened to a skeptical slate-gray when she heard his name. What mischief was this? Apparently her hope that Chandler was well out of her life wasn't to be. Well, so much for his promises! Turning to the twins, she said, "Please extend my regrets to Vicar Bromley and his wife for missing teatime. It seems there's still more business I must attend to concerning Father's will."

"Is Lord Leighton coming to see us?" Cecily asked. "I missed meeting him and I would so much like to!"

"No, I fear Lord Leighton is engaged in town, but no doubt you will make his acquaintance when—" The solicitor stopped abruptly. "I must speak with Lady Wythe before I can say any more on that head. I'm sure she'll discuss the matter with you when you young ladies return." He turned to Rosanna. "Might I make bold to suggest your sisters make use of my traveling carriage for their short journey? It would be more comfortable than this pony cart."

"Oh, please, may we use it?" Cecily pleaded, her eyes bright with excitement at the prospect of junketing about the countryside in such an elegant style.

Rosanna smiled. The Millbourne traveling coach was comfortable, but it lacked the dash of the one before them. "I suppose it will be all right. Lucinda," she winked, smiling warmly at the two excited girls, "see if you can keep your sister from making young Bromley stutter."

When they'd departed for the vicarage, she turned to face Mr. Crumbee, her smile gone. "Now sir, what business do we have? I thought I'd made it quite clear to Chand...to Lord Leighton that I wouldn't appreciate anyone meddling in our affairs. He seemed to agree." A hope glimmered. "You didn't find some other paper to overset Father's will, did you?"

"Unfortunately, no. Might we go inside? It is a private matter I wish to discuss."

That didn't bode well, Rosanna thought with a fr.
What nonsense was Chandler up to now? With a graceíu.
shrug she led the way into the house. A watchful Hobart
was standing in the entry hall. "Will you take tea, sir,
or do you wish something stronger?"

"Tea, thank you."

"Please bring it to the study, Hobart. Oh, and put
some of those apricot tarts on the tray as well if Cook
is finished with them," Rosanna directed.

Turning right, she entered the room where she'd first
seen the man who was embroiling himself far too much
in her life for her peace of mind. Blast him, why couldn't
he just leave her alone! But Rosanna controlled her
expression to show no sign of her inner turmoil as she
sat on the settee and motioned the solicitor to an adjoining
chair.

Leveling determined eyes at him, Rosanna inquired,
"May I know the nature of your business, sir?"

Crumbee, perhaps unused to having young ladies look
at him with such assurance, shifted uncomfortably in his
seat. "Lord Leighton extends an invitation to his wards,
and to you too of course, Lady Wythe, to stay at his
home in Grosvenor Square for a visit."

"He *what?*"

Crumbee repeated the invitation, but Rosanna wasn't
attending as a riot of emotions and thoughts flashed
through her mind. Unhappily, the first thing that popped
in was the memory of Chandler's stunned expression
when he'd seen Lucinda's beauty. She didn't forget his
comment about preferring fair-haired chits either! Was
he besotted by Lucinda? Was that why he wanted her
near? The idea twisted like a knife in Rosanna's heart.
She tried to recall if he'd shown any partiality to Lucinda
while they were dining. No, his manner had been most

correct. In fact, he had seemed a trifle bored. But then a rake would be skilled at concealing the direction of his interest! Perhaps she was being fanciful, but still . . . Oh blast it!

"Mr. Crumbee, I fear your trip has been for nothing. It is quite impossible for us to accept Lord Leighton's invitation."

The solicitor sighed in exasperation. "Lord Leighton warned me you might balk at the idea. He suggested I use reason first and then insist."

"He has no right to insist or—"

"There you are wrong. He wants you and your sisters in London without delay. As his lordship's legal counsel, it's up to me to inform you that it is his right to demand the attendance of his wards, if he should so wish. As you know, your father's will gives him that authority. To be frank, you have no say in the matter."

An angry flush warmed Rosanna's face. How dare Chandler act in such a high-handed manner! A furious retort was on her tongue when a discreet knock informed her that Hobart had returned with the tea tray.

Her hands were unsteady as she poured a dollop of cream into the cups then added the scalding tea. Handing a cup to Mr. Crumbee, she insisted, "When he was here, Lord Leighton made it quite clear he didn't wish to be saddled with the care of my sisters. His other interests fill too much of his time for that, or so he said. Why has he changed his mind? I believe it is my right to know."

"I am not privy to his lordship's thinking, milady. I am merely following instructions. He has placed the traveling carriage at your disposal for the trip. You're to be ready to leave in the morning."

"Tomorrow? That's absurd! Besides, we haven't

reached an agreement, sir, so presume none!"

Crumbee's frown deepened. "You are indeed a most headstrong young lady!" He set down his tea cup on the piecrust table at his side. "Lord Leighton warned me you would be," he muttered under his breath. He gave Rosanna a long, hard look.

From the expression on his face, she knew he'd decided to try a different tack. She was proven correct when his voice mellowed to a grandfatherly tone. "My child, why all this dust-up?" he asked with gentle kindness. "Most women would be delighted with the offer of a trip to London, especially one sponsored by the Earl of Leighton. Have you ever been there?" When she shook her head, he smiled and continued. "There are many educational things to see and do. Why, a visit to Lord Elgin's marbles alone is worth the trip!"

"Educational it might be, sir, but it would also be dangerous."

"Dangerous? I don't understand."

"I will be blunt. My sisters are quite lovely. They're also very young and unused to the world. That is the crux of the problem. Such beauty and innocence must be protected. Since we are without parents, I must be the one to do so."

"So, it's the proprieties with which you are concerned!" Crumbee chuckled. "How doltish of me not to understand. You need have no fear on that score, milady. Naturally you will be there to chaperone your sisters, but in addition Lord Leighton has invited his aunt, Lady Kittering, the dowager Duchess of Habersham, to share the season as well. It will all be most proper, I assure you."

With Chandler in the house, Rosanna doubted it! Before she could comment further, Crumbee continued.

"How can you deny your sisters a trip to London? Do you really wish them to be buried here in Somerset?" Doubt flickered inside her and he pressed home the point. "Lady Wythe, you almost seem afraid of this trip, but think well. I truly can't believe your parents would wish you to deny your sisters this treat."

His words struck very close to home. Was she trying to protect Lucinda and Cecily, or herself? Uncertain, she nibbled on her lower lip. Were all her protests the result of her own fear of London. Was she afraid to reside in the same house with Chandler, afraid his attraction might lead her to another heartbreak?

Her indecision must have been obvious, because Crumbee softened his tactics even further. "Milady, if you're still determined not to permit this trip, I can return to London and try to convince his lordship to allow you to stay in Somerset, but I would be less than honest if I didn't say it would be a shame to deprive your lovely sisters of this opportunity."

Before she could answer, Cecily came bursting into the study. Lucinda and Adrian followed at a more sedate pace. As they entered, Rosanna saw Adrian bow his dark head close to Lucinda's and whisper something that drew a happy smile from her.

"Young Bromley is down with the mumps so we couldn't stay for tea. Think of it, mumps!" Cecily giggled. "Only a mutton-headed dolt like him would contact such a childish ailment!"

"We met Adrian on our way back," Lucinda explained, letting her gaze wander back up to the tall man at her side. "He's come to teach us that new step. That is, if you're finished with your business, Rosanna."

Crumbee looked at her inquiringly. "Have you made your decision, Lady Wythe?"

Rosanna felt her throat tighten. She sighed, feeling all at once that her life was altering forever. For the best? For the worst? She didn't know.

"I suppose there is really no choice in this matter." She glanced at her two sisters. "Your guardian"—a most troublesome guardian, she added in her heart—"has invited us to London for a visit."

Cecily squealed and slapped her hands with delight. "London!" she breathed ecstatically. "Oh, Lucinda, didn't I tell you Lord Leighton had come to change our dreary existence!"

"When do we go?" Lucinda asked.

Her words were quieter, but Rosanna saw excitement glittering just as brightly in her eyes. She had been correct. Truly, she had no other choice. She would have to be the cruelest sister in history to deny the twins such a rare treat! As for herself, she would have to hope the lessons she'd learned from her marriage to Giles would protect her.

"Lord Leighton wishes us to leave as soon as possible, but with as much packing as we'll have to do, it may be the day after tomorrow before we can be ready."

"That shan't be necessary, milady."

"Excuse me, sir?" Rosanna looked at Mr. Crumbee in confusion. "I fear I don't take your meaning. What won't be necessary?"

"The packing, Lady Wythe," he explained. "Naturally, Lord Leighton has made arrangements to provide his wards with the proper wardrobes. Fittings have already been arranged with Monsieur de Montaigne, currently the most fashionable modiste in Bond Street. His instructions were that you are to be included as well."

That snippet of information threw Cecily into even greater transports. Her laughter echoed through the room.

"Oh Rosanna, it appears you shall have that wardrobe I was urging after all. I vow it's long overdue!" She giggled again and hugged her older sister.

The news didn't sit as well with Rosanna. She resented Chandler's arrogant way of rearranging their lives with nary a word to her. The stubborn tilt returned to her chin. They would go to London, but she planned to make it quite clear to him what she thought of his top lofty manner.

Adrian's quiet voice broke through her agitated musings. "It would appear the dance instruction must wait." He glanced at Lucinda and cleared his throat. "If I may venture a suggestion, I'd like to offer my services to escort you to London. You must pass through Finchley Common on the way, and rumor has it One-eyed Jas is out highwaying again. I'd feel better knowing you shall arrive safely."

"That's most unnecessary, sir," Crumbee argued. "Lord Leighton has provided two outriders as guards. The ladies will be well-protected, I assure you."

Adrian shook his head stubbornly. "By your leave, Rosanna, I still ask permission to accompany you. My sister has been begging me for a vast age to take in the London sights. This seems a prime time to accept."

Rosanna smiled, knowing well what he was about. He didn't want Lucinda romping about London without him. "Of course you may ride with us, Adrian. We'll welcome the company."

He grinned, gave Lucinda a last, lingering look, and bowed. "Good. Then I shall take my leave and wait upon you in the morning."

The solicitor was also on his feet. "I've reserved rooms at the Three Plumes in Salisbury, so I, too, must beg permission to depart. It would be best if we get an early start. Would eight o'clock suit your convenience, milady?"

Rosanna's heart balked at taking the final step. It would be so much easier if Chandler didn't haunt her every thought, yet there wasn't anything she could do to shut him out. Swallowing down the nervous lump in her throat, she nodded.

CHAPTER

Four

THE TIGHTNESS IN Rosanna's throat increased as the traveling carriage rumbled through the crowded streets of London. She hardly heard the twins' excited chatter as they peered out the windows at the passing sights. All her thoughts were spinning around her forthcoming confrontation with Chandler. Uneasy about his intentions, she was determined to find out why he'd extended the invitation. If he'd formed a *tendre* for Lucinda, they most assuredly would not remain in London!

Cecily's squeal of delight when they turned into Grosvenor Square and saw Chandler's town mansion dragged Rosanna out of her disturbed wonderings. With a tug on the arm, Cecily urged her older sister to the window for a look at Lord Leighton's imposing home. Like its neighbors, the massive four-story house sat almost directly on the street with only a narrow walk in front. Its Palladian facade, softened only by the window pediments, conveyed enormous strength and power. Just like Chandler, Rosanna thought.

Adrian swung out of his saddle and helped them to alight. He made no move to leave as Crumbee mounted the steps and rapped loudly on the door with the ornate lion-headed knocker. A butler, equal to Hobart in his starchy manner, appeared to admit them.

"Jervis, please inform Lord Leighton that Lady Wythe and his wards have arrived," Crumbee instructed.

"Certainly, sir." The butler bowed low. "Might I suggest that the library would be an appropriate place to await his lordship. If you would please follow me."

As they all walked toward the sweeping staircase leading to the second floor, Rosanna's eyes widened in wonder. She had never seen a more elegant home. Persian carpets in rich tones of terracotta, cream, and navy were scattered over the marble floor of the great entry hall. An enormous chandelier of cut Venetian crystal hung above their heads, and suits of armor stood silent guard as they passed.

The library wasn't quite so daunting. There were rich carpets underfoot and watered-silk draperies swagged back with gold cord at the windows, but the dark oak bookshelves lining every wall added a cozy touch. To Rosanna's delight, she found works by many of her favorite authors on the shelves and, contrary to many libraries she had seen, the books looked well read. Had Chandler cracked the pages? she wondered. It didn't seem likely.

They were there only a few moments before the door opened and Chandler entered, followed by a man with carroty hair and laughing hazel eyes. Rosanna's gaze swept over the stranger. He lacked Chandler's height and breadth, but made up for it with a more approachable expression. He was attractive, but it was Chandler who sent her pulse thumping uncomfortably. After he had left Millbourne Hall, she had tried to convince herself that she'd only imagined his devastating appeal. But she hadn't. She felt the same breathlessness now.

Chandler's glance flickered over the group. He smiled briefly at Rosanna, but his eyes narrowed when they encountered Adrian standing close at her side. Rosanna saw his hands clench as the two men exchanged stares, but no hint of anger colored his introductions. "Sir Ed-

ward Maitland, I would like to make you known to Lady
Wythe, my wards, Lucinda and Cecily Millbourne, and—
oh, yes, I believe it is Adrian, Viscount Cameron. You
know Mr. Crumbee, of course."

Chandler's smile broadened as he looked at the twins
standing demurely in front of him. One was dressed in
a sprig muslin gown of primrose and the other in a matching style of pale blue. "Now, as to which of these two
lovely ladies is Lucinda and which is Cecily," he continued, "I have to leave for you to guess, for I certainly
can't tell them apart."

Cecily, in the pale blue, dropped a graceful curtsy.
"My lord, I was the one away from home when you
called."

"Ah yes, Cecily. It's a pleasure to make your acquaintance. And how is young Bromley?" he asked with
a tilt to his eyebrow. "Were you successful in your ef-
forts?"

At first Cecily blushed, then she giggled when it became clear that he wasn't preparing a scold. "Indeed,
yes, it took a scant five minutes to make him stutter."

"Poor sport, surely. We must endeavor to find someone more worthy for you to practice on. Maitland, my
friend, perhaps you would volunteer."

"I would be honored!" Edward's hazel eyes kindled
with pleasure as he moved purposefully to Cecily's side
and engaged her in conversation.

Rosanna frowned. Chandler was getting on familiar
terms with her sisters entirely too fast for her comfort.
Her doubt about his intentions leaped painfully to mind.
This nonsense should go no farther. "My lord, I'm sure
my sisters are fatigued from the journey." she said. "Could
someone show them to their bedchambers?"

"And you milady? Aren't you fatigued?"

."Naturally, but I should like a few words with you before I retire." She held out her hand to Mr. Crumbee. "Thank you, sir, for seeing us safely here."

Turning to Adrian, she placed a friendly hand on his arm. Before she spoke she flicked a glance at Chandler. It pleased her to catch his grin turning into a frown as he watched them. "Your escort was much appreciated as well, Adrian. You're a most thoughtful neighbor. We shall look forward to your promised dance lesson. I'm sure his lordship will grant us use of his music room for an afternoon."

"Do I have permission to wait on you tomorrow to see how you have settled in?"

Before Rosanna could answer, Chandler said, "Tomorrow, I fear, will be a trifle busy for the ladies, what with fittings and all. Best make it another time, old chap."

She threw an aggravated glance at him, but didn't argue because Jervis had appeared at the door. The twins dropped another curtsy, then followed the solicitor and Adrian from the room. Edward, obviously anxious to seek a few more words with Cecily, hurried after them, leaving Chandler and Rosanna alone.

They were silent for a few moments as they looked at each other. She wished desperately that his towering presence didn't do such disagreeable things to her heartbeat. Trying to throw off her confusion, she plunged ahead. "Lord Leighton, there is something—"

"Ah, yes. I guessed from that stubborn glimmer in your eye that we might be back to a formal Lord Leighton and Lady Wythe stance. I'd hoped we had parted on better terms than that." His voice dropped as a smile curled his lips. "Didn't we . . . Rosanna?"

"That was before—"

"Before what?" he interrupted, obviously enjoying her

discomfort. "Before I kissed your hand? You didn't seem to mind at the time. In fact, you seemed to—"

A hot blush appeared high on each cheekbone as Rosanna hastened to correct his thinking. "Chandler, don't be tiresome. You know very well—"

"At least you haven't forgotten my name. I like to hear it on your lips."

"Will you be serious!" she snapped, almost angry that he wouldn't let her speak her mind. He seemed to delight in fencing words with her, and another time no doubt she would have enjoyed it as well. But not now. Unless she received some satisfactory answers soon, there would never again be opportunity for such sport between them! She realized uneasily how much she would miss his banter—even if it was but a rake's banter—should they have to return to Somerset.

"Your invitation, Lord Lei—I mean Chandler, was most unexpected. You seemed glad to be rid of us when you left Millbourne Hall. Then your solicitor showed up on my doorstep with instructions my sisters were to appear in London without delay. He had no satisfactory explanation for your change of your mind. Perhaps you will explain it to me."

"The invitation wasn't just for your sisters, Rosanna. You were invited as well, don't forget. Perhaps I simply hungered for another set-to with you. Your chatter is ever entertaining."

"Nonsense! Until you saw Lucinda you made it quite clear we were a burdensome responsibility you would rather not be saddled with. Then, when she arrived, you—"

In three strides he had crossed the room and grasped her by the shoulders. "What hen-witted gibberish is this?" he raged, giving her a rough shake. "Do you honestly think me capable of dallying with innocents? Heed my words well. Much of what is said about me is true, but I have never been accused of seducing schoolroom misses, and I never shall! If anyone is in danger, it is you. You seem a prime piece to warm a man's bed. Why not mine?"

Rosanna's heart was pounding but she refused to back away from him, even though his fingers were bruising into her shoulders. They stared at each other, icy blue eyes locked with stormy gray ones. The air between them crackled with tension.

"Remember, it is only the fair-haired chits you favor. You made that most clear!" Rosanna tossed her dark locks. "I have nothing to fear from you."

"I wouldn't be so sure of that!"

The dangerous glitter in his eyes gave warning, but before Rosanna could put her hands up against his chest to ward him off, he yanked her into his arms. Hard lips descended to plunder her mouth. It was so quick she had no time to raise her defenses. At the touch of his lips, an answering fire blazed up within her and for a moment her mouth softened and clung to his in willing surrender. Then she stiffened. She had given her kisses to a rake once before. Never again, she reminded herself, struggling to be free from Chandler's arms.

He released her instantly, then took a step back and ran a hand distractedly through his hair. They were both breathing a bit unsteadily as they faced each other. "Hell and damnation, Rosanna," he thundered, "why can you do this to me? I never meant this to happen. I should have had a better guard on my temper, but when we're together . . ." His voice trailed off. When he spoke again, some of his control had returned. "I don't know what it is between us. We are never together without ending up having a mill."

He reached for her again, but this time his touch was gentle as his fingertips traced lightly over where his hands had just grasped. "Forgive me? Please."

His soft voice melted away her anger. Her breath quickened a second time as the heat of his touch seared through the thin muslin of her gown. Her knees weakened as she felt the long forgotten ache of desire start to spread again through her body. No! It must not be! Why did it have to be Chandler who sent her pulse racing? His kiss meant nothing! As he'd said, his temper had gotten the better of his sense. She couldn't even condemn him for it, because from the first touch of his lips she'd been a willing partner in the kiss. With a hopeless shrug, she moved away from him.

"No, it's I who should ask your forgiveness," she admitted in a strained whisper. "My question was unpardonable. You had a right to take offense, and then, well . . . I fear we both acted a bit mutton-headed. Let us say no more. I daresay it's best forgotten," she added bracingly, even though she knew putting the memory of his kiss from her mind might not be possible. "Shall we return to the question, for I am still perplexed. Why the invitation?"

"Come," he suggested, taking her hand and leading her to the leather sofa. "Let's sit and talk. To be honest, it's not easy to explain, even to myself."

He seemed content to keep his hand in hers, but she pulled away from his warm touch.

Chandler smiled at her prim withdrawal, but he didn't tease. Instead, he explained, "I attended Almack's Wednesday and some, ah, person began to tell me—"

"A woman? Perhaps one of your flirts?" Rosanna interrupted, trying to force a return of her good humor.

"As a matter of fact, it was a woman, but that doesn't signify." He smiled enigmatically, leaving her second question unanswered. "What she said gave me pause." He shifted uneasily on the sofa.

Rosanna was amazed. Surely the expression on Chandler's face couldn't be embarrassment. She had seen arrogance, confidence, and rakish humor flash in his eyes, but never this. He seemed reluctant to continue and that was certainly a puzzlement. "A woman saying something to give you pause must indeed be a first," she commented, trying to prod a further explanation from him. "I'm aflutter to hear what it could have possibly been!"

Her teasing drew a smile from him and some of the tension eased out of the tight set of his broad shoulders. "Aflutter? You?" he retorted. "I'd be dashed surprised if you would be put aflutter even if Henry VIII himself walked through that door and named you wife number seven. If you recall, that was one chap who did favor dark-haired beauties. But enough of this sparring."

Chandlers's eyes grew serious. "It's embarrassing to admit, Rosanna, but I'm not proud of my attitude over your father's will. I don't know. I probably resented having any of my father's responsibilities descend upon my head, even though Lord Millbourne was always kind to me when I was a lad."

Again, when he mentioned his father, a flash of remembered hurt darkened his eyes. Rosanna started to reach out toward him to soothe away the pain, but then drew back. She wasn't sure enough of him or herself to offer such comfort. Instead, she retreated behind light banter. "Or, my lord, it could just have been the self-indulgent laziness of someone who doesn't wish his 'interests' interfered with."

Chandler chuckled, the frown gone. "Could be," he agreed with a grin. "In any case, as I was explaining, at

Almack's, Lady Pond—the lady I was speaking of—chatted on about satisfying propriety with a duty call and then shoving you and your sisters conveniently from mind. Her words made me see how selfish I had been. I'm not such a foppish dandy that I would walk away from duty. My troops knew they could rely on me. Lord Millbourne should expect no less. She also went on to say that you would no doubt descend on my doorstop with your sisters and—"

"And," Rosanna interrupted, "you thought you might as well get it over with."

"Will you please let me complete my own sentences? I thought nothing of the sort. I knew that, with your dashed streak of independence, you would never press the relationship. But that didn't relieve me of my responsibility. You and the twins were placed under my care, and so it shall be." He paused, then finished the explanation. "I want to present your sisters formally to the *ton*. Since the Season has already begun, I had to insist that you hurry to London. There, the explanation is done. Truly, my intentions couldn't be more honorable. You planned to leave if my answers did not suit, didn't you?" he asked, accurately assessing her thoughts. "Believe me, I want to do this for your sisters...and for you. Will you stay, Rosanna?"

She couldn't stop her heart from beating faster as his voice caressed her name. Something warned her that staying was dangerous, but could she endure leaving? Still hesitant, she said, "A presentation to the *ton*. It is a very kind gesture, but I don't know if Lucinda and Cecily are old enough."

Gentle fingers lifted her chin until she met his gaze. "They are almost eighteen, Rosanna. Do you truly want them buried in Somerset with no one but the local squires to pay them court?" His eyes grew more serious. "I don't want to bring up unpleasant memories for you, but it's obvious your marriage wasn't happy. If you'd had the town bronze of a Season in London, you might have been able to judge your husband's true stamp before it was too late."

He was right. She couldn't deny Lucinda and Cecily a chance to gain the experience she had lacked. Chandler must have read the decision in her eyes because his smile returned. "You'll stay?" When she nodded, he exclaimed, "I knew we could come to an agreement." When she didn't respond, he asked. "We do have a truce, don't we?"

Resolutely she pushed all doubts away. "Well," she teased, some of her good humor returning, "at least temporarily."

"Splendid! You had your chance for questions. Now I have one for you. Why did that most persistent viscount, who seems to be forever sitting in your pocket, think it necessary to ride guard to London? Weren't my outriders sufficient? I assure you, they were two of my most reliable soldiers from my days of chasing Napoleon through Spain."

One phrase he had used echoed through her mind. How very wrong he was about Adrian. She'd better straighten him out. "Adrian is not sitting in my..." she began, then stopped. Had there been just a glimmer of jealousy flashing in Chandler's blue eyes when he spoke of the other man? A silly idea surely, or was it? Was she foolish to hope? Still, there was no reason why she must explain everything to the fullest.

A soft smile curved her mouth. "I would like to think that Adrian is just a good friend who is concerned about me, about all of us."

"And when is this *good friend* leaving?" Chandler demanded impatiently.

Rosanna's eyes widened innocently. "Why, he isn't. His sister has invited him for a visit. Isn't that nice? He can share the Season with us. That will be a most comfortable arrangement, don't you think?"

"Comfortable for whom?"

"Why, for me and for you actually, if you would only think about it."

When he looked profoundly doubtful, she went on to explain, "You see, Chandler, you have your, ah, I believe you call them 'friends,' at Almack's. But I know no one in London, save yourself. With Adrian here, I shall have someone to stand up with for the waltzes. As you can imagine, I do so hate to be mauled about by strangers. You see, you shan't have to worry. Adrian is a most excellent dancer. You won't have to partner us at every moment, which must be a vast relief to you, to be sure."

His expression was unreadable as he reached for her hand. His lips brushed softly against the back, then he turned it over and nuzzled a kiss on the warm, sensitive inner part of her wrist. "I am not a stranger, and I assure you I will not maul you about the ballroom as a waltz plays."

She gave her hand a gentle yank to free it, but he wouldn't let go. Instead, he placed another kiss on the pulse beating so erratically in her wrist. "Promise you will save at least one spot on your dance card for your sisters' guardian."

Just then the library door popped open. A fiery blush swept over Rosanna's face as she looked up and saw the black-gowned figure standing there. Quickly she yanked her hand out of Chandler's grasp, but she knew the woman's sharp eyes had missed nothing.

"Nephew, have your manners taken leave and flown to the belfry? Lady Wythe must be longing for her bed-chamber after that tedious journey, and here you have her trapped in the library with nary a refreshing pot of tea or glass of ratafia in sight. She must be quite dragged out."

Before the woman had finished her scold, Chandler was on his feet. Reaching down, he helped Rosanna arise, then bowed to the older woman. "Lady Kittering, dowager Duchess of Habersham, may I present Lady—"

"Oh, stop all this formal stuff and feathers!" Lady Kittering ordered, rapping her cane sharply on the floor. "I know who she is, and, if she has anywhere near the sense she looks like she possesses, she knows of me. Come here, child. My name is Emmaline."

As Rosanna moved bemusedly to her side, the other woman continued to chatter. "I have met those two sisters of yours, my dear. Real top-drawer lookers, if an old woman can say so. You may be proud; you've done well. Won't have a particle of trouble getting a couple of eligibles to come up to snuff with offers for them. Now come on, my manners at still intact, even if Chandler's are wandering. I shall show you to your bedchamber and you can wash off your travel dirt. Then it's early to bed for you. We have a scandalously generous amount of my nephew's money to squander on Bond Street frippery tomorrow, which is always an enjoyable but exhausting business. You'll need your rest."

"A moment, please," Rosanna requested as Lady Kittering guided her firmly through the doorway. "That matter is one we haven't yet discussed."

She turned back to Chandler. "Your guardianship was most unexpected, and no matter what gallantries you speak, it must be burdensome. A presentation is enough.

It's unfair for you to be saddled with my sisters' wardrobes as well. My pockets are plump. Please let the reckonings be sent to me."

"Have you got bats in your cockloft, child?" Lady Kittering fussed. "Let the boy handle it. If he has the blunt to play deep basset at White's, he can deck out his wards in style, and"—she paused, her shrewd eyes taking in the details of Rosanna's unfashionable black dress—"some new finery would do for you as well. There, it's settled! We shall hear no more of it!" she insisted, taking Rosanna's arm and escorting her away from an amused Chandler.

After Rosanna was gone, his smile faded and was replaced by a frown. Dash it all! Whatever had possessed him to drag her into his arms for that kiss? He'd never been one to force unwanted attentions on a woman. They were usually more than willing to share a kiss, and more.

Remembering again the feel of the warm inviting softness of her lips under his, he wondered if his attentions had been unwanted. Was he wrong, or hadn't she responded, at least at first? No, he chuckled, he was the one who had bats in the cockloft if he thought that! It was a wonder the little hellcat hadn't planted him a facer! Shrugging away the question, he pulled the bell cord, summoning Jervis to bring his greatcoat. He would adjourn to Boodles.

As Lady Kittering led Rosanna down a long corridor, she noted that family portraits of the Hartwicks stretching back to Plantagenet times lined the gallery. At the far end of the hall hung an enormous canvas of a lovely woman done by the noted Gainborough. Rosanna stopped to look at it. Familiar blue eyes smiled down at her, and she turned to Lady Kittering. "It's Lord Leighton's mother, isn't it?"

"Yes, that was my sister. I still miss her dearly. She died as so many do, in childbirth. The late earl never recovered from her death. I think that's why he retreated so deeply into religion and why he and my nephew never—" She put an abrupt rein on her tongue. "Stuff and feathers! Why are we posing on about the past? Come, I've asked Jervis to serve us dinner in your suite so we can have a nice coz. There is so much I want to know about my nephew's most unexpected guardianship. Bound to do the boy good! He has too much time, too much money, and too many chits chasing after him. A bit of responsibility will better fill his hours."

After seeing the style of the rest of Chandler's home, Rosanna should have been prepared for her bedchamber but still she was awed by the splendor of the three-room suite to which Lady Kittering directed her. Lush Aubusson carpets in green, sky blue, and gold muffled their footsteps as they made a brief tour of the rooms. Watered-silk fabric of the same light blue covered the walls and gold silk draperies hung at the windows.

The furniture was a special delight to Rosanna. She disliked the ornate Egyptian-inspired Empire furnishings that had recently come into vogue from France and she appreciated the simplicity of these chairs and tables trimmed with only a few elegant ormolu enrichments. Emmaline watched Rosanna as she ran her hand over the rich satinwood of the escritoire. "No need to ask if your accommodations are acceptable. I can tell you're pleased. I am as well. This was my sister Amelia's suite. It's good to see her belongings out from under the dust covers."

Rosanna turned to her in surprise. "Do you mean this was Chandler's mother's bedchamber? But these rooms should be yours."

"Fustian! I'm just a guest here, as you are. We can't go about oversetting my nephew's orders. Besides, he knew I always stayed in the Rose Suite when I used to visit Amelia. No wish to change now. Come, let us collect those two lovely sisters of yours. Their chambers are directly across the hall.

"Oh, by the bye, Jervis said my nephew was off to Boodles tonight, so our dinner will be a hen party. Hope the boy has a good turn at the faro table," she added as she rapped on Lucinda's door.

Emmaline's calling Chandler a boy made Rosanna smile. She let her imagination ramble as Emmaline summoned their dinner. Chandler must have been a handsome child with his blond hair tumbled by the wind and his blue eyes wide with innocence. Yes, he would have been exceedingly handsome before that hard, cynical glint entered his eyes. She wondered what had caused it. The war, too many easy conquests, boredom? The rattle of the dinner cart being pushed by Jervis down the hall toward her suite interrupted her musings.

CHAPTER
Five

ROSANNA SAW NOTHING of Chandler the next day as Lady Kittering dragged them from one end of Bond Street to the other, gathering up scads of dancing slippers, kid gloves, shawls of silver tinsel and spider gauze, and selecting dashing straw chip bonnets. Their last stop was at Monsieur de Montaigne's. While he cast himself into transports over the twins' beauty, Rosanna walked to the other side of the shop to look at several bolts of fabric.

After much gentle haranguing and a few thumps of her cane, Lady Kittering had finally worn Rosanna down and she'd agreed to order a few new gowns for herself. But she was determined that they be quietly sedate. Something in lavender or gray would do.

She was fingering a bolt of pale lavender satin when a masculine voice spoke at her back. "That is a perfectly dreadful choice. It simply will not do at all!"

Was he speaking to her? She turned to see who else was about, but there was no one else at that side of the shop. Perplexed, she turned again and confronted the most elegant man she had ever seen. His dark brown coat was cut so perfectly that it fit smoothly over his shoulders without a wrinkle, his breeches and hessians were correct to a shade, and his cravat was tied in a complicated style she had never seen before. "Sir, I'm sorry, I don't understand. What won't do?"

"That insipid lavender. Dash it all, it most certainly isn't your color. If you have a gown made of that, you'll look like a drab little mouse. Is that what you want?"

Thinking he might be a town dandy on the strut, Rosanna said in a scathing tone that spoke clearly of dismissal, "What I wish is certainly none of your business!"

"By Jove, you're spirited as well as beautiful. I knew when I first saw you that you weren't the usual ninny-hammer. It will be a pleasure to take a hand in this matter."

Amused by his chatter in spite of herself, she asked, "What matter? Sir, I vow you are talking nonsense!"

Ignoring her exclamations, he looked down at the narrow gold band on her left hand. "Waterloo?" he guessed correctly. When she nodded, he curled his lip in fastidious distaste. "That battle was fought well over a year ago. If you're out of mourning, why do you choose to rig yourself in such a way that all your charms are most effectively hidden? You're far from being permanently on the shelf, you know!"

"Neither am I a chit making her first bow," Rosanna insisted. "I don't wish to cut an unbecoming dash! I'm here merely to lend my countenance to my sisters when they are presented."

His eyes swept quickly across the room to where Lucinda's and Cecily's blond heads were bowed over copies of some of Monsieur de Montaigne's sketches. "Indeed, two Incomparables, nothing less," he admitted. "But they provide no challenge, you see."

Following his glance across the room, Rosanna caught Lady Kittering's eye and wondered why she was staring at them with a glazed expression on her face. At least Emmaline wasn't throwing a warning frown, so Rosanna felt safe turning back to her most amusing companion. "And I do present a challenge?" She laughed. "How ungallant!"

"Not ungallant, merely truthful." The stranger rubbed a thoughtful finger over his upper lip as he studied her closely. "I have had some small experience with the matter, and I can assure you that dressing attractively is never in bad taste." His eyes were fixed on her face. "What are you afraid of? Why do you insist on playing the dowd?"

His question reminded Rosanna unpleasantly of the same thing Cecily had asked only a few days ago. Had she deliberately been doing that? Had it been in the back of her mind that if she attracted no man, she couldn't be hurt again? She wanted to scoff at the idea, but she couldn't. Wavering, she tried to demure. "At my stage in life, I don't think it is appropriate to—"

"What isn't appropriate," he interrupted impatiently, "is dressing like a black scarecrow! I shudder when I see someone so ill-clothed."

Something attracted his attention outside. Taking her arm, he guided her to the large windows fronting Bond Street. "Let me show you how a young widow should dress," he insisted, pointing to a woman parading down the sidewalk in a dashing walking dress of turquoise and tan chintz. "Lady Pondesbury lost her husband in the war as well, but she isn't wearing the willow. As you can see—"

The rest of his lecture was lost to Rosanna, for her attention was riveted on the man attending so closely to the lovely widow's side. Even though his head was lowered to catch the lady's words, there was no mistaking the broad expanse of Chandler's shoulders. Rosanna's hands curled into tight knots as she saw Lady Pondesbury nestle a hand possessively in the crook of his arm and flutter her wide blue eyes up at him in, what seemed to Rosanna, a most insufferable way. Recalling the slip Chandler had made by saying "Lady Pond—" Rosanna knew that this must be the woman whose words had convinced him to tender the invitation for them to come to London. One look at the woman's blond beauty also answered the question about whether or not she was one of Chandler's flirts. There was no doubt of that!

Militant determination filled Rosanna as she watched them walk away. Her attention returned to the man at her side. "You must admit I'm right," the gentleman continued. "The lady dresses with flair, doesn't she? Why do you want to resist being equally well-clad?"

Rosanna refused to examine too closely her motives for her change of heart, fearing she might have to admit how much she truly wished to gain Chandler's attention. Swallowing back a doubt that she might be setting herself up for a fall, she agreed. "Sir, you are most correct. It is long past time for me to come out of these drab weeds. May I be so bold as to ask for your help?"

Looking pleased with himself, the stranger nodded. "I am ever at your service."

"Wonderful! If we're to be conspirators in this transformation, shouldn't we exchange names?"

The gentleman bowed elegantly from the waist. A slight smile twitched at his lips as he announced, "Mr. George Brummell."

"*The* Mr. Brummell? Beau Brummell?" she gasped, feeling a warm blush suffuse her cheeks. No wonder Lady Kittering had appeared so stunned when she'd seen them deep in conversation!

"I've been called that, but I prefer George. Might I have the honor of your acquaintance? I wouldn't forget so attractive a lady, so I suppose you must be new to London."

Still a bit overwhelmed at conversing with the famous arbiter of the *ton*, Rosanna stammered, "I am Lady Wythe, Rosanna Wythe. Lord Leighton is my sisters' guardian."

"Ah, yes, I believe I did hear Leighton had acquired some wards." He glanced across the room. "He should be delighted. They shall set the *ton* in a spin, and, with my help, you'll cause your own stir. A dashing widow is always intriguing. Lady Pondesbury has been without a rival for far too long."

Before Rosanna could comment, he urged, "Come, we have much to do. Lady Jersey is an old friend of Lord Leighton's. I trust she has sent vouchers for Almack's. You must plan on making your debut there."

"But that is the point." Rosanna objected. "Lucinda and Cecily are being presented, not I."

"Enough of this. Consider it your coming out of mourning and let's hear no more. Monsieur"—Brummell lifted an imperious finger—"leave those young ladies to one of your assistants and join us. Any pastel gown will do nicely for them, but a master's hand is needed here."

The designer was reluctant to abandon the twins, but Rosanna knew Brummell's summons couldn't be ignored. Monsieur de Montaigne's trained eye swept over her drab clothes and unstyled hair as he crossed the shop toward them. His twisted smile showed he was far from impressed.

"You are the sister of those two?" the little Frenchman demanded once he'd reached their side.

"It may be hard to believe, but I am," Rosanna admitted, beginning to doubt the advisability of Brummell's plan. "It may be difficult, but perhaps—"

"What is needed is a gown for Lady Wythe that will set the *ton* in a whirl," Brummell interjected, not mincing words. "A new fabric, a new style, something different from the mode. The word in Bond Street is that you are the best. If this is so, you should have no trouble."

The Frenchman inclined his head to accept the compliment. "An intriguing problem," he murmured, walking around Rosanna. "Mmmm. There is one possibility, ah, but no, I forgot. That bolt of fabric is promised."

"What fabric is this?" Brummell demanded.

The other man shifted uneasily from foot to foot. "My friend, Joseph Jacquard, is only now getting back into silk production after that monster Napoleon made him convert his looms to weave wool for uniforms. One—I repeat—only one length of his unique fabric has reached these shores, and I have promised it to Lady Pondesbury."

When Rosanna heard the name, she insisted, "Let's see it."

"But Monsieur, Madame, it's not possible."

"Very well. If you don't wish our patronage," Brummell drawled, "I am sure Chatwick will welcome it. Lady Wythe, may I escort you to his shop?"

"Wait!" The Frenchman twisted his hands. "Oh, very well. It shall be." He looked Rosanna over, a creative gleam starting to glow in his eyes. "Not in the mode, you say? I believe...yes, I think it will be *magnifique!* The color was all wrong for Lady Pondesbury in any case. I will have to tell her a little fib, but you shall have the fabric."

He shouted a few words in French and an apprentice came running with a length of the most beautiful fabric Rosanna had ever seen. The silk was a rich ruby red and woven in such a way that its subtle paisley pattern caught and reflected shimmering light. "Ah yes." Monsieur de Montaigne sighed, draping the fabric over her shoulder. "I'm glad Lady Pondesbury won't have this. Look how it makes this lady's eyes sparkle. And if we cut this hair short, we can—"

"No," Rosanna snapped, remembering how she had sheared and crimped her locks to please Giles. "I like my hair long and so it will stay."

"I think you are correct," Brummell vowed. "Gently curled and accented with red roses instead of jewels, your hair should be smashing with the ruby gown. Milady, we have contrived well this day. I shall look forward to your triumph at Almack's. Now I must take my leave. The Prince of Wales is expecting me at Carlton House."

Brummell took a wrapped parcel one of Monsieur de Montaigne's assistants brought over. Looking at it, he wrinkled his nose, then glanced back at Rosanna. Obviously thinking of his reputation, he explained, "Please don't refine too much upon finding me here. I don't usually frequent dress shops, even fashionable ones in Bond Street, but His Highness heard Monsieur had received a new shipment of fabric from China. Naturally the Regent wouldn't rest until he'd badgered me into coming down here to pick up the samples for that blasted Pavilion of his."

Rosanna smiled. "The reason you were here doesn't matter. I'm simply grateful for your help. Thank you again."

"I'm always delighted to help a beautiful woman become more beautiful." He bowed and started to leave, but turned back with one final instruction. "Remember, Monsieur, keep the lines of the gown simple. Possibly some trim at the hemline, but that should be enough.

Lady Wythe herself will do the rest." With another bow, he was gone.

The instant Brummell was out the door, Lady Kittering and the twins rushed over to find out what he and Rosanna had been talking about. "My dear, what a stroke of good fortune!" The older woman beamed after hearing what had transpired between them. "Honestly, I can't guess why Brummell professes such an interest, but he is always a creature of whim. You can count yourself lucky. A bow from him will assure the success of your sisters, to say nothing of your own hopes."

"I have no hopes other than to see Lucinda and Cecily happily established," Rosanna insisted.

Yet when Monsieur de Montaigne started drawing quick sketches of the gown he intended to create for her, draping the gorgeous silk this way and that about her slender body, she knew she'd lied. There was scant use in denying it. She did have a hope, that Chandler would look at her as something other than an amusing companion with whom to fence words.

Reminding herself time and again that he was nothing but a rake mattered little to her heart. Those words had no power to compete against the memory of his kiss. Even now she hungered for another touch of his lips. Was there any chance of that when he already had the fair-haired Lady Pondesbury at his side? Rosanna glanced again in the cheval glass and marveled at how the lustrous ruby fabric accented her eyes. Maybe, just maybe, there was a tiny chance.

She turned impulsively to the Frenchman. "Monsieur de Montainge, I'm growing fond of this color. Could you make me a riding habit of velvet in the same shade?"

"With a black collar and lace jabot, no?"

"Perfect. And you'd best add some sort of hat, please."

Rosanna's smile deepened. "Maybe one with a saucy feather. For the first time in a long time, I feel in the mood for something frivolous."

"Milady"—he bent over her hand—"I am glad Monsieur Brummell's eye is unerring. He never fails to spot a jewel, even if it is hidden under dowdy black. Now I shall do my part. Your gown, into which I will put my very soul, will be delivered soon. As for me, I ask but one thing." He placed a dramatic hand over his heart. "Please promise your hair will find some curl before the ball!"

Several days later, Rosanna looked in the mirror and laughed, remembering the dressmaker's request. If he could see her now, with dozens of linen strips wound in her hair trying to coax some curls into the stubborn locks, he might change his mind. Dropping her towel, she stepped into a hot bath. The scented water swirled up around her, filling the air with her favorite lilac fragrance.

It was hard to believe that five days had sped past since their arrival in London, five days of endless shopping and introductions, five days since Chandler had kissed her so unceremoniously. Rosanna had seen little of him since that day. He had appeared twice at dinner, but was usually from home. Was he spending those hours with Lady Pondesbury? With a sigh, Rosanna settled deeper into the hot bath and tried to think of the evening ahead where Lucinda and Cecily, under Lady Jersey's kind patronage, would make their bow at Almack's.

She was stepping out of her bath when Cecily burst into the room. "Rosanna, look. These flowers just came for you. Do you have a secret admirer?"

"What a tiresome question. Why must you always have such romantic imaginings? You know I don't have

any admirer, secret or otherwise. The flowers are probably from Lord Leighton. I believe that is a customary
gesture."

Cecily shook her head stubbornly. "No, the flowers
he sent came earlier. Lucinda and I received pink rosebuds and you got violets that will clash horribly with
your new gown. He probably thinks you'll wear gray or
lavender or some other insipid shade. I do believe our
guardian will be quite surprised at your new dash! May
I open the box, please? I'm aflutter to see who's sending
you such a gift." As she tore away the paper, she chat-
tered, "Maybe it's from someone who has seen you from
afar and is sending a tribute of his love. Wouldn't that
be romantic?"

Rosanna shook her head. Still, she had to admit she
also was eager to see what was in the box. Nestled in
the green tissue were three perfect ruby red roses. On
the card was written in a bold hand, *'From dowd to
dazzling. Save me a waltz.'*

So the famous Brummell hadn't forgotten their chance
encounter. Rosanna was pleased. "Cecily, please ring for
Kate to come help me dress. You had better start getting
ready yourself."

Before leaving, Cecily gave her older sister a hug.
"Tonight shall be such fun. I already have three places
filled on my dance card, and we aren't even at the ball
yet. Adrian wants a cotillion, his lordship has requested
the first country dance, and that handsome Edward Maitland has asked if he can stand up with me for a quadrille,"
she explained, yanking on the bellpull. "You know, I
thought he was quite shy, but he isn't at all."

"Who did you think was shy?" Rosanna asked, un-
winding the linen curlers. "Surely you don't mean Lord
Leighton?"

"Silly goose, of course not! I mean Mr. Maitland."
A delicate blush tinted Cecily's cheeks. "You remember,
the man with that wonderful red hair. He has called once
or twice to see how we are getting on. I believe you were
taking tea with Lady Jersey the last time he was here."

"Obviously a most considerate young man," Rosanna
commented absently. "Now you had best hurry."

Kate arrived to brush out Rosanna's heavy mane of
hair. As odd as they'd looked, the linen curlers had turned
the trick. Her hair tumbled down her back in lustrous
dark curls. A few concealed pins held the curls in an
elaborate chignon and the three ruby roses, nestling among
the locks, added the perfect splash of color to accent the
dress Monsieur de Montaigne had designed for her.

The silk was sensuously soft to the touch, and Rosanna
luxuriated in the feel of it, even over her undergarments,
as Kate helped her carefully into the gown. Rosanna
looked in the cheval glass, finding it hard to believe this
strikingly lovely woman was the same drab mouse who'd
buried herself in Somerset. As Brummell had suggested,
the rich trim was confined to the hem of the dress, where
a wide band of embroidery shimmered like a golden river
as she walked.

"Rosanna dear," Lady Kittering called from the hall-
way, "are you dressed enough so that I might come in?
I have something for you." She entered carrying a flat
velvet box. Her eyes lit up with approval as she inspected
the younger woman. "I must say you're in excellent looks
this evening, but I believe there's one thing that might
improve this pretty picture. Here," she said, handing the
box to Rosanna. "I haven't worn these in a vast age, but
I think they'll suit."

Inside was a magnificent ruby and diamond necklace.
As she stared at the glittering jewels, Rosanna couldn't

say anything at all. "Lady Kittering, I can't possibly wear these," she protested finally.

"Stuff and feathers! Emmaline snapped, allowing no argument as she clasped the necklace around Rosanna's slender throat. Before Rosanna could properly thank her, Lucinda and Cecily joined them. Rosanna smiled with quiet pride. Were there ever two lovelier girls? Both were dressed in tulle, Cecily in ice blue and Lucinda in green the color of seafoam. Tiny satin rosettes accented their demure bodices. A simple strand of pearls at the neck and the pink rosebuds in the gold filigree *bouquetiere* Chandler had sent completed their outfits.

"Ladies," Lady Kittering said, beaming, "it puts me in a high gig to be able to present you to our friends in the *ton*. I haven't had such fun in years. I'm delighted that old crosspatch of a brother-in-law of mine was friends with your papa. Shall we go?"

As they descended the sweeping staircase, Rosanna saw Chandler standing in the great entry hall with Edward Maitland. Suddenly feeling shy, she hung back and let the other three go ahead of her. Chandler's greeting to his wards was correct and complimentary. Then he turned to her. A confident smile curved her mouth when she saw the undeniable flare of interest in his blue eyes. His lips lingered on her hand.

"I can see that my choice of violets was quite out. You should have sent word. I'm sorry you had to purchase your own flowers for this special evening," he apologized.

Pulling herself away from Edward's compliments, Cecily informed him pertly, "Oh, Rosanna didn't buy those. They came just an hour ago with a note."

"An admirer?" Chandler asked, the hard glint in his expression hinting that he didn't like that possibility at all. His eyes raked over Rosanna's figure, caressing the firm curve of her breasts, which were revealed enticingly by the cut of her bodice, before he demanded again, "Well? Who is your admirer?"

"The note wasn't signed. They're probably just from a friend," Rosanna commented casually, trying to pretend that the warmth of his gaze didn't fill her with longing. To cover her confusion, she concentrated on adjusting the shawl of gold lace tinsel draped over her arms.

"You seem to have quite too many 'friends,' milady!" Chandler vowed with a dark frown. "We'd best go. I'm sure you wouldn't want to keep them waiting!"

She smiled blandly at him. "I agree. That is so tedious, don't you think? No doubt there are a number of fair-haired misses most anxious for your appearance as well." Batting her thick lashes, she murmured so that only he could hear, "I'm convinced you wouldn't wish to keep Lady Pondesbury waiting any more than I would my friends." Without a backward glance, she delicately lifted the hem of her skirt and started for the doorway.

Edward's eager conversation with Cecily covered the tense silence that stretched between Chandler and Rosanna as they all rode toward Almack's. When they alighted form the carriage in front of the famed marriage mart, Chandler drew Rosanna aside. "I shouldn't have crossed swords with you, especially not tonight. Please accept my apologies. I want this evening to be very special." His blue eyes swept over her again and he smiled. "I don't believe I told you what fine looks you are in tonight, milady." Holding out his arm to escort her inside, he vowed, "It will be an honor to present both you and the twins to the *ton*."

"You're devilish handsome yourself, my lord." Rosanna's dimples flashed as she tucked her fingers into the crook of his arm. "For an old soldier, that is!"

Rumor of Leighton's beautiful wards had already swept through the *ton*. An expectant hush fell over the dancers as they were announced. Without really being aware of it, Rosanna searched the crowd for Chandler's Bond Street walking companion. She finally spotted Lady Pondesbury gaily holding court across the floor. Like almost everyone else, she was straining to see the twins.

At the first sight of Lucinda and Cecily, Rosanna saw Elvinia relax. Obviously Lady Pondesbury had feared that they would be competition, but was reassured to find them little more than schoolroom misses. Then Rosanna's own name was announced. Stepping forward, she delighted in watching the expression on Elvinia's face harden into a decided pout. Even from across the room, Rosanna could tell that the slender ivory sticks of Elvinia's fan had snapped beneath her angry fingers. Confidence flowed through Rosanna. Maybe Brummell's chatter about her rivaling the fair Lady Pondesbury wasn't such nonsense after all.

Rosanna's smile widened further when the other woman's furious glare swept over her ruby gown. There was no mistaking the unique Jacquard weave. From the look in Elvinia's eyes, Rosanna knew that Monsieur de Montaigne would have much to answer for. Elvinia was definitely not pleased!

Rosanna felt quite the opposite. The evening promised to be a complete success. Chandler's gleam when he looked at her, his telltale jealousy over the roses, and most of all the undoubted triumph of Lucinda and Cecily, made her happy. Her glance rested on Chandler's broad shoulders as he escorted Cecily out to the set forming for a country dance. She owed him many thanks. He could so easily have left her and her sisters in Somerset and not have taken the trouble and expense of a bow to the *ton*. It was a most generous and unselfish gesture.

Rosanna's pleasant reflections were interrupted by a touch on her arm. She turned and smiled at Adrian. "If we step briskly," he suggested, holding out his arm, "I think we have time to join that set with the twins."

Rosanna reached up on tiptoe and whispered in his ear, "I tried to save this dance for you with Lucinda, but some young buck cut you out."

Adrian grinned down at her and chucked her gently under the chin. "You're incorrigible! Is it so obvious how I feel about her?"

"Only to me, and that's only because I care so much for both of you." She gave his arm a reassuring squeeze. "Now let's not tarry. My dancing slippers are itching to do some steps."

Chandler's eyes locked with hers as she and Adrian joined the group forming for the dance. Rosanna realized that years of command had steeled him to show little of his displeasure, but the tightening of his square jaw betrayed him, telling her he hadn't missed her bantering interchange with Adrian. She smiled serenely at him, then fluttered her lashes most provocatively at Adrian. Letting Chandler think she welcomed Adrian's attentions wouldn't hurt at all!

As soon as the music ceased, all three ladies were surrounded by eager suitors for places on their dance card. The twins might have received a bit more attention, but Rosanna was certainly not lacking for partners. Chandler and Adrian were left to one side. "Your choice, Cameron, was certainly better than mine," Rosanna overheard Chandler comment. "My violets were left in a vase at home while she's most publicly sporting your roses. My congratulations."

Adrian stared at him, puzzled. "I thought the pink roses were from you. Lucinda told me—"

"The *pink* roses are," he interrupted. "The red roses Rosanna is wearing are not. I thought—Do you mean you didn't send them either?"

"No." Adrian chuckled. "It would appear that Lady Wythe doesn't lack for admirers. If you will excuse me, I believe a waltz is next."

Having overheard this exchange, Rosanna was flushed with pleasure. She saw Adrian start toward her and turned to find Chandler walking step for step with him. Both men reached her side at the same time. Adrian bowed. "May I have the honor of—"

"Sorry, old chap," Chandler intervened, putting his arm about Rosanna's waist. "All her waltzes are bespoke by our previous arrangement."

The music began and Rosanna was whirled out onto the floor before she could object. "Have you run mad?" she protested. "What is this nonsense about bespoke waltzes?"

Chandler's arm tightened, drawing her closer into his embrace. The pressure of his touch sent tremors of desire through her and she yearned to be closer to him.

"Your memory must be quite faulty," he whispered in a low voice, his warm breath tickling her ear. "You most clearly said you detested being mauled by strangers. The only honorable thing to do was offer my services."

"Adrian is not a stranger!"

"Merely a small detail," he said with a shrug, then whirled her about so fast that she was flung deliciously against him. Rosanna was quite breathless by the dance's end, but whether it was from the spirited step or Chandler's presence, she wasn't sure. She only knew she hated for the dance to end.

The hours passed in a whirl as partner after partner

demanded Rosanna's hand for dances. Even Brummell managed to pry himself away from the Regent's side to beg a turn on the floor with her. His lavish compliments on the success of their plan filled her with pleasure. Ever mindful of her sisters, she asked if he might stand up with them as well, and was pleased when he agreed.

But most special of all for Rosanna were the waltzes she danced with Chandler. With each opening note, he appeared promptly to claim her. As the music spun its magic around them, she nestled deeper into his arms. On a turn at the end of the ballroom, the muscular strength of his thigh brushed hard against hers, sending far-from-innocent desires bolting through her body. The degree of longing his touch kindled thrilled her, yet at the same time made her vastly unsure. No wonder the older dowagers still looked askance at the waltz, she mused as the pull of his arm dragged her even nearer. It ignited such tempting fires that were not easily resisted.

CHAPTER
Six

ONLY TWO THINGS dimmed Rosanna's pleasure that evening. After one waltz, she and Chandler found themselves at the end of the ballroom. Both breathless, they hardly noticed Wilbert until they had practically walked into him. Rosanna felt Chandler's grasp tighten protectively about her bare arm when he saw Giles's cousin.

For Rosanna it was far from a welcome encounter. She wanted no reminders of Giles or her marriage. She edged instinctively closer to Chandler, glad to have his strength and support by her side.

"Ah, I see you've returned from Somerset." Chandler's tone sharpened ominously as the two men confronted each other. "Rumor has it the climate can be as dangerous here as there, if one isn't careful. Best remain properly removed," he stated, making pointed reference to his warning to stay away from Rosanna and his wards.

"Have I a choice, Hartwick?" Wilbert challenged with a surly growl.

"No more than Napoleon did when I led the charge at Talavera."

A few more acrid barbs flew, then Wilbert stomped off. Rosanna stifled a sudden shiver. What was it about Giles's cousin that make her skin prickle with unease? Perhaps it was simply his squat, toadlike appearance that put up her hackles, but she wasn't sure that was all.

Pushing all such imaginings aside, she glanced up at Chandler. "My lord, it seems I must be forever thanking you for standing between me and my husband's family."

"All part of the Hartwick guardianship, Rosanna," he joked. Then he sobered. "I'm glad I was here. Even without that dreadful puce waistcoat, the man is obviously a nasty piece of goods. You shouldn't have to handle the likes of him alone."

Before they could speak further on the matter, Lord Jersey came to claim his minuet. With effort, Rosanna shoved the disagreeable memory of Wilbert from her mind and determined to enjoy the remaining hours of the ball. For the most part, she succeeded. The only other encounter that marred her pleasure occurred when she saw Chandler leading Lady Pondesbury onto the floor.

She retaliated by adding an extra flirtatious sparkle to her laugh whenever Chandler's eyes rested on her during the dance. It was a delightful game; a game that, since she'd married so young, she'd never been able to play. Luckily, the technique came easily as she fluttered her lashes most provocatively up at her partner and was rewarded with a thundering scowl on Chandler's face.

Rosanna also found a chance to converse with Chandler's friend Edward Maitland. Impressed with his quiet strength, it pleased her to see him dancing attendance on Cecily. If only her sister could see his worth, but that was doubtful. In the past Cecily's taste, much to Rosanna's disapproval, had run to men with more dash than value. It was a bothersome problem

Near midnight another waltz was played, and Rosanna welcomed the opportunity to dance with Chandler again. When the waltz was over, Elvinia glided over to where Rosanna and Chandler were standing. Placing a possessive hand on his arm, she cooed, "Milord, please introduce me to your wards' older sister. I hear she is recently up from the country." At the word "country," Elvinia wrinkled her nose delicately as if she could still smell the horse droppings clinging to Rosanna's shoes.

Chandler's grimace suggested he was torn between amusement and exasperation as he glanced from one to the other. Finally he shrugged. "Lady Wythe, I would like to make known to you, Lady Elvinia Pondesbury."

Elvinia, obviously eager to put the countrified Rosanna in a fluster, said in her sweetest voice, "Lady Wythe, pray don't take this amiss, but honesty impels me to speak a word of warning about your gown. La, if I didn't have such regard for Lord Leighton, and your dear sisters, of course, I would never venture to say anything on the matter at all; but I'm convinced you wouldn't wish to put them to blush. To be quite frank, that gown simply is not up to snuff. The color, I fear, attracts undue attention, and the severity of the line certainly isn't in the mode. While you're not a green-goose, to be sure, I know you are new to London and wouldn't wish to make a mistake."

While Elvinia was rambling on, Rosanna kept the same innocent smile on her face, but her rapidly tapping kid slipper, just visible beneath the hem of her gown, warned of an impending dust-up. "How very thoughtful of you to share this warning with me," Rosanna answered in a tone as sugary as Elvinia's. "Isn't she kind, Chandler? I must fetch Mr. Brummell and tell him his taste is quite out. He'll be as disheartened as I that—"

"Brummell!" Elvinia squeaked. "What does he have to do with this matter?"

"He had a most direct hand in designing my gown. It's a pity I shall have to tell him you think his taste is not of the mode. He seemed quite certain I would be properly gowned, but if you say—"

"You can't tell Brummell that!" Elvinia insisted,

twisting her hands nervously. "A set-down from him
would quite ruin everything. You have misunderstood
me. It isn't Brummell's choice of style that is question-
able," she vowed, trying desperately to wriggle out of
the mess she'd fallen into. "It's that fabric, you see, that
is so unusual."

"Indeed it is," Rosanna interrupted with a satisfied
smile. "I was most lucky to get it." She looked directly
at Lady Pondesbury. "Can you imagine, some blond miss
had the abominable taste to insist she wished the length
for herself? I'm sure you'd agree that would never suit."

Chandler, apparently deciding he'd best intervene before the two ladies ended up with drawn claws at ten
paces, siezed the opportunity provided by a lull in the
music to interrupt. "Ladies, the evening is growing quite
warm. May I fetch you an iced lemonade?"

"Chandler, you are so thoughtful, or"—Rosanna smiled
knowingly at him—"at least occasionally so. But I think
not." She turned to the other woman. "Lady Pondesbury,
it was so, ah, interesting meeting you. I would adore to
stay and chat, but I must go in search of Mr. Brummell."
She looked back over her shoulder, locking eyes with
Chandler. With an impertinent toss of her head, she announced, "Oh, by the bye, the last waltz is reserved for
him."

When Rosanna reached Brummell's side, he nodded
toward the couple she'd just left. "What did you do to
that pair? Hartwick is frowning like a thundercloud, and
Lady Pondesbury's pout would sour cream. Did you flip
the tables on our dashing widow?"

"Oh, I think she's merely miffed because the fabric
she wanted was used for my gown," Rosanna answered
somewhat vaguely. She was distracted far more than she
cared to admit by the sight of Elvinia flirting outrageously

with Chandler. Her smile faded as she watched him respond to her seductive smile and the touch of her fingertips as they trailed suggestively up his arm.

Luckily, Rosanna couldn't hear their conversation or she'd have been even more displeased. As Brummell led her out onto the floor, Chandler's full attention returned to Elvinia. "My waltz is free, my lord," she murmured. "Would you care to dance with me? I won't shunt you aside as Lady Wythe did so rudely." Lowering her voice to a more intimate level, she whispered, "I do so love to be in your arms." She glanced about the crowded ballroom and sighed. "Almack's is so dreadfully public. La, I yearn for a few private, completely private, moments with you." She looked coaxingly up at Chandler, an open invitation sparkling in her blue eyes. "Now that those tedious wards of yours are established and Lady Wythe has so obviously found her feet, couldn't we plan that outing to Hampton Court?"

"Hmmm . . . Hampton Court. A splendid idea," Chandler murmured, looking across the floor to where Brummell and Rosanna were laughing together. "I must admit the thought of secluded glades is suddenly vastly appealing. Shall we set next Saturday as the date?"

"Oh, yes," Elvinia agreed, gloating. "Saturday will be perfect. Although I'll find it most difficult to wait."

The music began again. "I believe this is our waltz, milady." Chandler bowed.

As the music played, both couples whirled about the room. Brummell was an excellent dancer, but Rosanna felt none of the disquieting thrill she'd experienced in Chandler's arms. Her partner smiled down at her. "You have the tongues wagging tonight, Lady Wythe."

"Yes, indeed." Rosanna nodded. "Lucinda and Cecily have made quite a success, but I knew they would."

"Lady Wythe, you aren't attending. I said you—not your sisters—are the center of much ado. Everyone is intrigued by your unique gown and how you twisted your lovely long hair into such an unusual style. I believe you might set a new fashion." Brummell's fastidious glance swept over the swirl of dancers. "And it's about time! All these ladies with their close cropped and curled hair look like so many bobbing Greek statues. It's becoming most tiresome."

"Sir, I think you are talking nonsense, but I still thank you for the compliment. I also must thank you for the roses. As you suggested, they provide the perfect finishing touch. Lord Leighton was most interested to discover who sent them."

"By Jove, I trust you didn't tell him." Brummell chuckled. "A woman should always have an unknown admirer about to pique the interest of the other men. Let the roses be our secret," he added with a grin as the final notes of the waltz faded away. He tucked Rosanna's hand in the crook of his arm and started across the floor. "Before the evening concludes, I must pay my respects to Lord Leighton."

The two men exchanged bows, then Brummell drawled, "My compliments, old chap. I had no idea the bet could be won so quickly. Whether you claim the pot for introducing this lovely lady here to the *ton*," he commented, bestowing a warm smile on Rosanna, "or for your two smashing wards makes no difference. No one could possibly best you."

"What is this about a bet?" Rosanna asked warily.

Elvinia eagerly sketched in the details. "It was Mr. Brummell's most excellent idea," she gushed. "Being bored with the insipid crop of chits being popped off this season, he issued a challenge to see who could produce the belle of the *ton*. La, it's the most famous thing that

Lord Leighton has won! Wasn't a monkey at stake, milord? Whatever shall you do with all your winnings?"

A bet! Chandler had brought them to London for no other reason except to win some vulgar wager! Rosanna's hands curled into tight knots, but, aware that Almack's wasn't the place for dagger drawing, she held her tongue. "How amusing, to be sure! My lord, you must tell me all when we arrive at your house!"

There was an edge of steel in her voice that Chandler couldn't miss. His expression revealed that he knew they were in for a prime set-to this time. "I am ever at your service when you wish words, milady." He bowed stiffly. "Now I believe we'd best collect Lucinda and Cecily and take our leave. Lady Kittering is nodding over her lemonade."

The twins, thirlled with the excitement of the evening, didn't seem to sense anything amiss on the carriage ride home, but Rosanna saw the concerned looks Lady Kittering cast as she glanced first at her nephew then back to her. Rosanna was sorry to worry her.

The moment they all entered the house, Rosanna turned to Chandler. "I will have that word with you now, my lord! Let me see my sisters to their chambers, and then I'll meet you in the library." Without waiting for his assent, she started up the sweeping staircase.

Chandler was pouring his second glass of brandy as she entered the library a few minutes later. She shut the door behind her with a furious snap. They stood facing each other.

"Rosanna, I want to—"

"Lord Leighton, I don't appreciate being played for the fool," she interrupted. "That happened once before, and, well, I was hen-witted enough to actually believe you were different! That makes me doubly a dolt. I should have learned that your type never changes."

"My type? I suppose you're comparing me to your husband? If you do that, you indeed earn the label 'hen-witted.' How can you think—"

"What I think is that you've had your sport at our expense. It doesn't matter to me, but I think it's monstrously cruel to Lucinda and Cecily! You have raised their hopes, but now you mean to end it. And I actually thought to thank you! Your noble words about duty and responsibility meant nothing!" Rosanna raged, overwhelmed with anger. "All of this was merely to win some ill-bred wager! Well, sir, you've had your fun and won the bet. When do you expect us to leave for Somerset? Will your coach be available, or shall I rent a traveling carriage? Never fear, we shan't be a bother. Adrian will be more than willing to ride guard."

"I'm sure he would!" Chandler avowed with a dark scowl. "He seems more than willing to do any of your bidding, but it shan't be necessary."

"What do you mean? Surely you don't expect us to travel on a public stagecoach?"

"Don't be addle-brained! I would never allow that, and you know it. You aren't leaving London in any type of carriage. You aren't returning to Millbourne Hall."

"Have done, sir! The game is played. There's no reason to pretend you want us to stay here. We shall be ready to depart in the morning."

"You little fool!" he growled, advancing toward her. "What do I have to do make you listen? A shake helped once before. Shall we try that again?"

He towered above her, the powerful thrust of his shoulders making Rosanna realize why many of the *ton* called him untamed and untamable. But her pride wouldn't allow her to back down. "I wouldn't advise you to lay a hand on me, my lord."

"Hell and damnation, Rosanna, what would you sug-

gest then?" he demanded, rubbing a hand across his forehead. "You won't let me explain."

"Any explanation would only be more untruths. Save
us the bother and admit you wish us gone."

"I wish you gone, do I?" Chandler fumed. "If I wished
that, would I have arranged to have Firefly brought to
London so that you could ride him? If I wanted you
gone, would I have organized an outing to Hampton
Court for a picnic next Saturday? Rosanna, believe me,
I knew of the bet. I was there when that damned Brummell made it, but I honestly didn't bring you and the
twins here because of it!" He reached out to her, and his
touch was soft, not rough. He pulled her gently toward
him. "I wanted you with me in London. I wanted Lucinda
and Cecily to have their Season, and you as well. I
honestly had forgotten about the dashed bet until Brummell, ever eager for deviltry, reminded me of it this
evening."

Rosanna looked up at him wonderingly. Could he be
telling the truth? Her heart prayed anxiously. Surely he
wouldn't have made such plans if he'd meant only to fill
his pockets with some wager funds. But she had to be
sure. A trembling smile deepened her dimples. "Is Firefly
really coming?" she whispered.

"Yes, you silly child. I told you before, I don't lie.
He'll be here tomorrow. Bucephalus and I eagerly await
another gallop with you." A spark ignited his blue eyes.
"Truly, I don't wish you to leave. The Season would
seem most flat if you weren't about to joust words with
me, to say nothing of the fact that I would lack for a
waltzing partner." He pulled her closer into his embrace.
"You do fit so nicely into my arms."

"And the bet, Chandler?" she asked, wanting the last
little doubt removed.

"Dash the bet! I won't claim my winning, and that

shall finish the business. Brummell can look elsewhere
for the belle of the *ton,* even though I truthfully don't
think he could find a better choice than the woman I see
before me. I know I mentioned it before, but you do
look vastly fetching tonight."

Rosanna felt her eyes crinkle with laughter. "You
don't think my gown calls undue attention to me, my
lord?" She peeked flirtatiously up at him. "Lady Pondesbury's comment cut me to the quick."

"You little minx." He chuckled, his hands moving up
and down her bare arms in delightful strokes. "If anyone
was cut, it most certainly wasn't you. For no doubt the
first time in her life, Elvinia was bested. And as for her
gibberish about calling attention, as beautiful as you look,
you rate a goodly number of stares!"

Rosanna was finding it extremly difficult to breathe.
They were standing so close that her bodice almost brushed
against his chest. His clean, rugged scent filled her senses
and urged her closer into his arms. Their eyes met and
her lips parted in response to the fire in his gaze. Chandler
lowered his head. His soft caressing lips stroked over
her mouth once, twice, evoking an answering need deep
within her. But before the desire could be sated, a sharp
rap made them spring apart.

Lady Kittering peered around the edge of the door,
then walked in. Her sharp eyes swept over the rosy blush
on Rosanna's cheeks and a smile curved her mouth, but
she made no comment. Instead she admonished, "Chandler, my boy, it has grown late. Lady Wythe should be
in bed. She'll be fatigued into a decline if she doesn't
find her chamber soon."

He picked up Rosanna's hand. "Are we of one mind
on this matter now, Lady Wythe?"

"Indeed we are. But if I might suggest, why not claim

the wager money and give it to your vicar? I'm sure he could find a good use for it."

"Splendid idea. But since it's the Millbourne ladies who have won the hour, with your permission I shall send it to Vicar Bromley. Then hopefully we'll hear no more of it. Brummell's jest has caused quite enough trouble." He kissed her hand. "I bid you goodnight."

"What is this stuff and feathers about money and vicars?" Emmaline demanded, leaning on Rosanna's arm as they slowly ascended the staircase.

Her laughter rang out as Rosanna told her the tale. "Were you terribly vexed with my nephew, my dear?" the elder woman inquired as they reached their bedchambers.

"Indeed, I was," Rosanna admitted. "May I be frank?" When Lady Kittering nodded, she continued, "I fear Chandler's reputation may have caused me to think the worst when I heard about the bet. Somerset is admittedly a backwater. Still word of his set has reached even there." She paused, trying to put her feelings into words. "Yet when I'm with him, he seems kind and considerate and—Oh, I don't know. It's a puzzlement."

Lady Kittering patted her hand. "Come, my dear, keep me company for a while. I think it's time you knew more about Chandler."

When they were settled on the settee by the fire in Lady Kittering's suite, she began to explain. "My nephew was a delightful little boy, always eager to please. Yet no matter how hard he tried he could never satisfy his father. The late earl was always finding fault, always condemning...always, I felt, unjustly. His growing religious fervor seemed to consume him." Her eyes grew misty. "I don't think he ever forgave Chandler for the death of my sister. He loved Amelia passionately. After a while, Chandler simply gave up. He couldn't do anything to win his father's love or approval, so I think he decided to prove his father right. You have heard the rest."

Rosanna nodded. "His amorous adventures. Yes, I know. His father used to moralize about them at our dinner table."

"I certainly won't say Chandler's rakish reputation was unearned. That would be a mighty Banbury tale indeed! Yet there are two things I wish you to consider, Rosanna. His rules, in their own way, are most honorable. No one can say he dallies with innocent misses or leads anyone on with an expectation he'll come up to scratch. And let us be honest. He didn't earn his reputation all by himself. Women have pursued him from the moment he made his first bow. Can you blame him for tasting of the fruit so freely offered?"

Remembering the kiss of the moments just past, Rosanna blushed to the roots of her hair. Was that all she was to him, just a ripe peach or plum to sample? It was a lowering thought. But was it truly the same between them? She'd had a rake's kisses pressed on her lips before and this felt so different! She felt tenderness and a caring in Chandler's touch that went beyond simple passion. Was she indeed a fool to hope? Or was Chandler deceiving her cleverly with a raffish skill even greater than her dead husband's? If only she knew.

Patting the younger woman's hand again, Lady Kittering commented, "My dear, you don't have to answer my question about Chandler's reputation. Perhaps I shouldn't have spoken so plainly to you, but I wanted you to understand about my nephew. All I'm really saying is that there is a good, brave, reliable man under all his *tonnish* bronze. His military record proves that. I choose to think this is the real Chandler, not the bored rake who winds his way through the herd of *tonnish* ladies. I assure you, bringing you and your sisters to London merely to win a bet is something he would never do."

Lady Kittering raised a scolding finger. "Now off to bed. Remember we have a musicale to attend at Lady Bigge's tomorrow. Best prepare yourself. That daughter of hers will screech out a tune while playing most miserably on the harp. At times like those I'm glad I'm a bit deaf!" With a quick kiss on the cheek, Lady Kittering ushered Rosanna out of the door toward her own bedchamber.

The older woman's words gave Rosanna much to think about as Kate helped her change out of her ball gown. It was late, but a drowsy feeling refused to come. Rosanna curled up by the fireplace in her velvet wrapper and gazed into the dying flames. Lady Kittering's explanation cleared up so many mysteries about Chandler. She couldn't excuse his rakish pursuits, but at least now she understood why he had kicked so hard against the narrow rules dictated by his father. How could she condemn that? In her own less rebellious manner she'd done the same thing when she'd insisted on wedding Giles.

In one way Lady Kittering had eased a few lurking fears. Somehow Rosanna had sensed Chandler wasn't the wild libertine painted so vividly by the gossipmongers. It was comforting to have someone confirm her reading of him. In another way, learning such things made him all that much more dangerous to her. Even before she knew the truth of his character, his appeal had lured her toward dangerous feelings. Calling him a profligate rake had afforded her some protection. Now that protection was crumbling.

Long minutes crawled by as Rosanna's muddled thinking spun round and round, finding no answers. Frustrated, she stood up. Such ramblings were useless. Remembering the enticing array of books in the library, she decided that reading might help shut out the bothersome emotions that were making sleep so impossible.

The house was silent as she made her way to the library. She opened the door and was startled to see Chandler sitting behind the massive desk. "Ah," he said with a smile, "another nighttime prowler. Do you feel as restless as I this evening? Shall we blame it on the scent of spring in the air?"

The informality of his brocade satin and velvet dressing gown made Rosanna feel self-conscious. She drew her own wrapper more firmly about her. "I didn't know anyone else was awake."

Chandler laughed at her obvious discomfort. "Why are you hovering about the door? Come in. I promise there is no reason to be skittish. I reserve my library for activities other than seduction."

"Oh? And what about earlier this evening?" she retorted, recalling their kiss vividly.

"Everyone deserves at least one momentary lapse," he commented, ignoring the issue as if the kiss had meant nothing to him.

Leaving the door wide open, Rosanna took a few hesitant steps into the room. She glanced at the papers and books scattered over the polished surface of Chandler's desk. "I'm sorry if I'm disturbing you, but I couldn't sleep and thought a book might help pass the hours."

"Any disruption is most welcome. I'm certainly not making much progress on this project," he admitted, gesturing ruefully at his notes. "With all the recent gadding about, I've fallen behind on my work and thought

I would use these hours to finish a speech I must deliver Friday in the House of Lords on the Ireland question. It's such a thorny knot, I fear it will never be untied."

He turned over a few pages in one of the open books. "I thought comparing Rousseau's tracts with those of that colonial, Thomas Paine, might give me some ideas, but none have come." He arose and walked from behind the desk. "I know you wouldn't be interested in such heavy reading, so I'll see what else I can find on these shelves."

His airy dismissal of her interests piqued Rosanna. In her sweetest voice she said, "Yes, tonight I believe I do fancy something a bit lighter, although from time to time I quite enjoy batting around Burke's philosophy versus those of the revolutionists. I find Rousseau's ideas somewhat unrealistic. What do you think?"

Chandler raised a surprised eyebrow. "I think I must be sponsoring a bluestocking into the *ton*. What an intriguing mind you have hidden beneath that pretty head."

"A woman doesn't have to be a bluestocking to think and to be interested in the world."

"Touché!" He grinned most engagingly at her. "How odd. I don't think I've ever before conversed about politics with a woman in the middle of the night. It's certainly a different way to spend such time, an interesting change. Now let me see what I can find for you to read."

Why must he always confuse her so? Rosanna fumed silently as he glanced over the shelves. She knew what he usually did with a woman in the dark of the night. Part of her couldn't deny that she yearned to feel that type of passion from him while part of her delighted they could talk easily just as friends. Blast and double-blast the man! The longer they were together, the more complex and dangerously appealing he became to her. She sighed. With any luck the twins would soon be estab-

lished and she would retreat to the safety of Millbourne
Hall.

Finally he pulled a well-worn volume from the shelf.
"Ah, I've found just the thing." He handed the book to
her. "The plays of Molière. They saw me through many
a tedious night in Spain. He's a bit scandalous in parts,
but as Lady Pondesbury phrased it so impolitely, you're
no green-goose. It shouldn't put you to the blush."

Rosanna looked down at the book in her hands. How
wrong he was. When she looked at him, unable to still
her fiery response, she felt very much the green-goose.
And a hen-witted green-goose at that. A few tears prickled behind her eyelids. Mumbling a quick thanks, she
turned and left.

Chandler's feelings were equally muddled. He sat at
his desk a long time after Rosanna was gone without
putting quill to paper. He frowned as he tried to understand the vague discontent that had been plaguing him
of late. Impatient fingers drummed on the arm of his
leather chair as he mulled over the matter. Rosanna evoked
so many moods within him. Why? He'd jerked her into
his arms for a hard kiss. He'd acted a dolt over those
blasted roses. He'd felt fiercely protective when Wilbert
had blocked their path this evening. Shrugging away the
confusion, he decided he was merely bored. It was difficult to settle back in the *tonnish* whirl after his years
in the military. Lady Wythe was simply an interesting
diversion. Yes, he nodded, picking up his pen, that's all
there was to it.

Rosanna's light scent lingered about him. He inhaled
deeply again, comparing it to the heavy tuberose fragrance Elvinia doused on herself. Lilacs, that's what it
smelled like. They suited Rosanna. They were softly
beautiful, just like she'd felt in his arms when they'd

waltzed. His thundering frown returned. Hell and damnation, where had that noddycocked thought come from? Assuredly there must be bats in his cockloft! He went to the window and threw it open to get rid of the disturbing scent. Yet for some odd reason his frown didn't lift as he returned to the writings of Thomas Paine.

CHAPTER
Seven

TRUE TO CHANDLER'S promise, Firefly arrived the next day. Rosanna was feeding him bites of apple when Adrian rode up. "I see an old friend has joined you. Shall we go for a gallop in the Row?" he suggested.

"Is a gallop in the Row proper? I thought a lady was supposed to promenade sedately, so that everyone could admire her newest bonnet," she teased.

"Don't wear a new bonnet, and then it won't matter. Hurry and change. Firefly is already pawing impatiently to be off."

Rosanna needed no more coaxing. While Adrian paid his respects to Lucinda, Rosanna sped up to her chamber to don her bottle-green riding habit. The other new one from Monsieur de Montaigne hadn't arrived yet. She crossed her fingers and hoped that the ruby one would arrive before their outing to Hampton Court.

Rosanna felt good riding Firefly again. Naturally, cantering through crowded London streets was far from a mad gallop across the lawns at Millbourne Hall, but it was better than sitting primly in a barouche with a frilled parasol held most properly to shield away every ray of the warming sun.

The Row wasn't nearly as crowded as when the *ton* promenaded on Sunday afternoon, but there was still a fair number of carriages making the circle. Riding side by side, Adrian and Rosanna trotted about once, nodding to acquaintances. In one group of carriages she spotted Brummell and Lady Jersey conversing with Lady Pondesbury. They drew rein to exchange greetings.

Rosanna smiled at Lady Jersey. "I want to thank you again for allowing Cecily and Lucinda the treat last evening at Almack's."

"My dear, we should thank you for introducing two such lovely young ladies to the *ton*. They enlighten an otherwise dreadfully dull Season. Isn't that so, Elvinia?"

"La, you are most correct. Lady Wythe, you shouldn't have a bit of trouble establishing them most credibly. Then you can return to Somerset," she added waspishly.

"What foolishness is this? We can't have one of the jewels of the Season quit London!" Brummell jested, obviously pleased that his deviltry was oversetting the all-too-sure-of-herself Elvinia. "But if I might venture"— he winked at Rosanna—"a jewel in ruby would be more pleasing."

"We are in agreement, sir. It's on order," Rosanna assured him.

With a bow she and Adrian rode on. A few more paces brought them to the back curve of the promenade. Stretching in front was a long, clear path to the gate. "Do we continue being dully proper, or shall we have a run at it?" Adrian challenged.

"Have you ever known me to turn down a gallop?" Rosanna laughed, tapping Firefly firmly on the flanks.

Upon arriving back at Grosvenor Square, the riders received a chilly reception. Adrian was helping Rosanna to alight when Jervis opened the front door for Chandler's exit. As once before when Adrian's hands had spanned Rosanna's waist, Chandler's blue eyes darkened. "I believe the first gallop with Firefly was reserved for Bucephalus," he commented harshly.

"Was that our understanding, my lord? I thought you were referring to a gallop during our picnic on Saturday. Oh, by the by, might Adrian accompany us?" Rosanna's eyes were wide with mock innocence. "The twins would find that most enjoyable."

"Certainly, if you wish it," Chandler agreed surlily with a thinly disguised growl. "He can also entertain Lady Pondesbury, who'll be joining us as well."

"How delightful for you." Rosanna smiled sweetly, refusing to let him see how that bit of news clouded her good spirits.

Their eyes met, both of them totally ignoring Adrian. "I bid you good day, milady." Chandler nodded curtly. "The debates in Parliament claim most of my time. It's doubtful if I will see you before Saturday morning. No doubt Cameron will keep your day from becoming too tedious."

"You may be sure of it, my lord," she retorted.

When Chandler had left, Adrian asked, "What was all that nonsense about? The chap acted jealous. He doesn't think I'm sitting in your pocket, does he? That would be a good jest!"

"With Lady Pondesbury hanging on his sleeve, I'm sure Chandler has no time for jealousy."

"But he seemed most—"

"No, Adrian, I don't want to hear any more about it. Let's go inside and discuss the plans for our picnic to Hampton Court. I hear they have a maze." She forced a laugh. "Perhaps you can arrange to get lost with Lucinda!"

"That's a most appealing thought." Adrain chuckled.

As Rosanna had hoped, the ruby velvet riding habit

arrived Friday from Monsieur de Montaigne. The matching hat, styled à la Hussar, was nestled in the bottom of
the box and its dashing looks pleased her. She placed
it on her dark, tumbled curls and delighted in the way
the saucy black feather bobbed when she tossed her head.
She slipped into the rest of the habit. The severe lines
of the jacket molded over her figure, revealing its curves.
If only Chandler noticed. She sighed, no longer trying
to deny his appeal. The habit's final touch was the lacy
jabot that made a feminine ruffle at the jacket's black
velvet collar.

The next morning Rosanna shook away the nagging
wish that Chandler hadn't invited Lady Pondesbury on
their outing, picked up the long skirt of her habit, and
entered Lucinda and Cecily's chambers. Since they
planned to travel in the barouche instead of ride, they
were attired in attractive morning dresses of batiste accented with sprays of embroidered lovers' knots.

Rosanna smiled at them, but a sad thought tugged at
her heart. Lady Pondesbury was most correct. With their
beauty and tempting dowries the twins were bound to
settle on husbands soon. Then there would be nothing to
keep Rosanna in London. The thought brought such a
wistful look to her face that Lucinda asked with concern,
"Rosanna, are you unwell? You look sadly drawn. I'm
not sure this frolic is wise. Hampton Court has been there
since Tudor times. It will be available another day for a
picnic."

Even Cecily commented on her pallor. "You don't
look well, but I should hate to miss the fun. Our guardian
said delightful Mr. Maitland will accompany us. Nevertheless, I agree with Lucinda. I think you should take to
your couch."

"What ninnyhammers!" Rosanna teased, forcing back

any hints of sadness. "You are imagining things again. I am fit and ready to romp."

Cecily giggled. "While you're romping, why not romp a step or two on that Lady Pondesbury. With her high-flown airs, she deserves a come-down!"

Rosanna tossed an admonishing frown toward Cecily, then noticed that Lucinda's concerned gaze still rested on her. "Truly, I am fine!" she reassured her sister. "I believe I'm just pining a bit for Millbourne Hall. Rusticating at Hampton Court will, no doubt, put me back in fine fettle."

A rumble of male voices floating up from the entry hall told them it was time to depart. To Rosanna's surprise, in addition to Edward, Adrian, and Chandler, Neville Tweedsmuir was there. Had he been invited as a companion to Elvinia or was he there to keep Rosanna occupied while Chandler dallied with the blond widow? Chandler gave Rosanna no clue as he directed Jervis and a footman to gather up the hampers of picnic fare.

Outside, the carriage and three horses—Rosanna's, Chandler's, and Adrian's—awaited the party. As the grooms brought the horses forward, Bucephalus suddenly took violent exception to Adrian's horse. Angry whinnies split the spring morning air and hooves flashed as the two stallions prepared to do battle. The grooms dropped the reins and shied back, obviously afraid to struggle with the powerful animals. Muttering an oath, Chandler strode between the two rearing horses. He reached out and with one commanding yank on the reins firmly called both horses to order. Only then did the cowering grooms rush forward to tend their charges.

"Cameron, old chap," Chandler called as he stroked Bucephalus's neck, "our horses seem to have no fondness for each other. Unless we want another dust-up, might

I suggest you travel in the barouche as well? There should be room since Rosanna and I are riding."

Adrian smiled agreeably at the chance to spend several hours at Lucinda's side, directed that a groom tend to his horse, and climbed readily into the carriage.

Chandler's hands felt warm and strong as he tossed Rosanna into her saddle. She smiled down at him. "How strange that Bucephalus took Adrian's horse into dislike. He and Firefly seem to deal well enough together."

"I don't find it strange at all. Bucephalus has excellent taste."

Rosanna frowned at him in bewilderment. What did he mean? Then her heart delighted when she heard him mutter under his breath as he swung into his own saddle, "Like master, like horse. I share much the same feelings for his owner."

As Rosanna suspected, Lady Pondesbury's establishment in Mayfair was most impressive. Her husband had certainly left her comfortably plump in the pockets. Rosanna tried, but she couldn't keep her fingers from tightening on the reins as Chandler entered the mansion to wait on Elvinia. Her ominous presence was the only element darkening the proposed outing.

Lady Pondesbury was obviously no happier than Rosanna about the matter. A pouting frown flashed across her face when she walked outside on Chandler's arm and found the crowded barouche. Apparently, Rosanna mused, Elvinia had thought she and Chandler were to have an afternoon alone. Yet, skilled in flirtation, Elvinia let Chandler see none of her pique as she laid a possessive hand on his arm. "I am so sorry your wards foisted themselves onto our private day. It makes me vastly unhappy that the secluded glades will have to wait."

Rosanna's back stiffened when she heard Elvinia's

seductive invitation. There was no doubt in Rosanna's mind what kind of treat Chandler could anticipate when he and Elvinia were alone. He started down the steps, but Elvinia held him back. "Let's pray that someone comes quickly up to scratch so that you can get rid of your tedious charges," she continued in a voice so low that only Rosanna and Chandler could hear. "I'm sure that Lady Wythe is yearning as much for a return to Somerset as I am for her to go." Then with a sugary smile, Lady Pondesbury climbed gracefully into the carriage, taking a seat beside Neville.

Keeping a steady hand on their horses as they rode through the noisy streets held all of Chandler's and Rosanna's attention. Chandler made no attempt to converse with Rosanna as they followed the barouche out of London. Once beyond the city, they cantered along the Thames River out toward Hampton Court. Around one sweeping bend lay the palace, sprawling across its green park. Rosanna was thrilled as she regarded the red brick square clock tower guarding the entrance.

Chandler glanced at her and grinned. "I would say old Henry VIII did quite well when he snatched this pile from Cardinal Wolsey, wouldn't you? Legend says he honeymooned in this palace with five of his six wives. Only the Spanish Catherine wasn't bedded here. It's obviously a good place for romance."

"Oh, really!" Rosanna retorted with a teasing toss of her head. "Considering what happened to four of those five wives, I think I'd rather find my romance someplace else."

"Ah, I keep forgetting your little bluestocking mind." He held up a restraining hand. "And before you cast a frown at me for calling you a bluestocking again, I meant only that you have obviously read history. It's a pleasure to find a woman who thinks of things other than what gown to wear to the next ball."

Their banter was interrupted when the driver drew the barouche up under a shady tree and everyone alighted from the carriage. Adrian headed for Rosanna to lift her down from her saddle, but Chandler, dismounting rapidly, bested him.

She slid willingly down into his arms and for a few precious seconds Chandler's hands lingered about her waist. They stared into each other's eyes for a breathless moment, then Elvinia's chiding voice recalled their attention. "Milord, the drive gave me a thirst. Did you bring lemonade or, more delightfully, champagne?"

"If I know Jervis, he packed both. Everyone, attention please," Chandler continued in a louder voice. "Shall we delve into the hampers and lay out the spread, or do you wish to walk through the gardens before we dine?"

The consensus was to explore the hampers. Elvinia removed herself regally as the others scattered the linen tablecloths on the ground and laid out the wide array of food. Chandler's chef has spared no effort, even though it was merely an alfresco feast. A chilled baron of beef jostled beside three pigeon pies. Boiled lobsters nestled in among a green salad. Plump oysters were mixed with clams and scallops in a spicy red sauce, and to end the meal, there was a meringue basket filled with iced petits fours. Rosanna marveled that it had arrived in one piece.

The only sour note was, as usual, supplied by Lady Pondesbury, who fussed, "La, that sun is most distressing. Milord"—she batted her lashes at Chandler—"might I beg you to adjust my parasol? I don't dare let the sun touch my skin or I'll be burned as red as that lobster." While he complied, she commented to Rosanna, "You are so fortunate, my dear, to have dark hair. Why, with your skin tone, those freckles hardly show at all! I must be so careful. The least little touch of sun and I must bathe my face in cucumber juice."

Knowing what was coming, Rosanna threw a warning glance at Cecily, but it was too late. "Best be careful, Lady Pondesbury, that all that cucumber juice doesn't turn you into a pickle!"

Elvinia raised an eyebrow at Cecily's impertinence, then looked directly at Rosanna. "Too bad the *ton* didn't have time to realize that your sisters were versed in making ill-mannered remarks before they agreed Lord Leighton had won Brummell's wager. But then, it was such a vulgar bet anyway. I don't suppose it matters."

Rosanna had been about to scold Cecily herself, but Elvinia's words stopped her. Meeting the other woman's gaze coolly, she challenged, "I hardly think it is vulgar to be proclaimed a beauty, or, in this case, a double beauty."

"True," Elvinia nodded, fanning herself regally. "I was the reigning belle the year I made my debut, but no one was ill-bred enough to bet money on it."

"I fear Lady Pondesbury has indeed had too much sun, Chandler. She just called you, Mr. Brummell, His Highness, and others ill-bred. Surely she wouldn't have said anything so outrageous if she were not unwell. My heavens, look at her. Her face is the color of a beet. Perhaps a cold compress would help," Rosanna suggested, sweetly solicitous.

"Lord Leighton, you aren't..." Elvinia sputtered, trying desperately to wiggle out of the trap Rosanna had led her into. "I did not mean you were ill-bred...Ah, it's only wagers I disapprove of."

"There I must agree with Lady Pondesbury," Rosanna said, turning her attention to Chandler. "Usually wagers are not to my liking either. They seem so foolish. But in this case, when you've so generously agreed to match the money you won in that donation to Vicar Bromley, I have to admit that the wager will do much good. Lady Pondesbury, don't you think that was generous of his lordship to give all that money to our parish?"

A haughty sniff was all the answer she got from Elvinia. An awkward silence stretched between the two women. Finally Edward rose to his feet. In an obvious attempt to melt the ice-tinged air, he reached down a hand and helped Cecily rise. "There is a marvelous maze built of shrubbery on the far side of the palace. Shall we challenge your sister and the viscount to a race for the center?"

"What fun," Cecily giggled. "Come on, Lucinda, Adrian." With that, the four of them took off across the park for the gardens.

Neville Tweedsmuir looked adoringly at Elvinia. "You do look a bit peaked, milady. Might a stroll through the rose garden help? It's not in full bloom yet, but enough buds are open to make an attractive walk. Or if you wish, we could visit that maze. You would be out of the sun there."

Elvinia glanced eagerly at Chandler, obviously waiting for him to lay rival claim to her time, but he said nothing. She raised her hand delicately so that Mr. Tweedsmuir could help her to her feet. "I certainly have no wish to get lost amid a bunch of shrubbery, but a stroll to view the roses would be nice." She threw a challenging look at Chandler before returning her attention to the hovering Neville. "I hear your rose garden at Tweedsmuir Manor is the loveliest in England. You must tell me about it. No doubt it cost a pretty farthing to establish." Elvinia put on her most seductive smile.

"Chandler, won't you join us? Oh, and of course, Lady Wythe, you're welcome, too."

Before Rosanna could answer, Chandler spoke for them both. "The gardens shall have to wait for another day. Lady Wythe and I have other plans."

"Well," Elvinia pouted, "we most assuredly wouldn't wish to intrude upon your plans. *Isn't it convenient she is way beyond the age of needing a chaperone!*" With an irritated flounce, she grabbed her parasol. "Neville, are you coming or do you also have plans with Lady Wythe?" Rosanna heard his stammering disavowal as he and Elvinia started down the gravel path toward the rose garden.

Rosanna stifled a delighted giggle at Elvinia's obvious displeasure and began gathering up the picnic fare to repack in the hampers. "Rosanna, leave that and come here," Chandler instructed. "The groom will tend to it after he's had his own meal."

She suddenly felt shy as she sank down on the linen tablecloth beside him. What foolishness, she thought, to be in such a fidget. They were in a public park so why feel hesitant about enjoying his company?

"What was that gibberish you were spouting to Lady Pondesbury about my matching the amount of Brummell's wager? This is the first I've heard of it."

Rosanna smiled blandly at him. "Didn't I mention there was a penalty for your making such an outlandish wager? It must have slipped my mind."

"Nothing slips your mind! It's too sharp for that. But since you've committed me to the money, I'll pay it." He poured out the last of the champagne into two glasses. "It's worth that and more to have the twins, and you, in London with me. Shall we make a toast to the rest of the Season?" he suggested, handing her one of the glasses.

When she hesitated to take it, his smile faded. "Don't you like champagne, Rosanna? I noticed you drank only lemonade with the luncheon."

"To be honest, I've never tasted it before," she admitted. "It always seems to make a person frightfully difficult to deal with and—"

"I think I understand. You don't need to say anything more. On top of everything else, Giles was often foxed as well. I can see why you have a distaste." Very deliberately he poured the wine onto the grass. "I won't force you to taste it. How about our gallop instead? That's the next most intoxicating thing I can think of besides bandying words with you."

"You know I'm ever game for a race. I haven't had one since—"

"Since you put the Row in a spin by galloping down the back promenade," he completed. "You needn't look so surprised. Word of your escapade was running like fire through White's a scant hour after you thundered out of the gate."

"Were you put to the blush? I'm sorry, but I just couldn't resist."

"I should have been! Half the *ton* was scandalized. The other half applauded your daring, to say nothing of your riding skill. Luckily Lady Jersey and Brummell took the latter side, so your reputation is still intact." He shook his head as he gazed at her, then reached out to stroke the curve of her cheek gently. "You are an impetuous creature. Someday that will, no doubt, lead you into trouble. Let's hope I'm about to bail you out."

His touch was far more heady than any champagne could ever be. Rosanna felt a warmth flooding into her face, making her almost dizzy with longing. For one breathless moment, she thought he was going to kiss her, then his hand dropped to her wrist, pulling her up with him as he got to his feet. "If we don't ride soon, our guests will be back. I'm quite sure Lady Pondesbury won't be content for long amid the roses, even with the rich Tweedsmuir at her side."

Behind the palace was another expanse of green parkland that led into a wooded area near the Thames. Firefly needed little urging to break into a powerful gallop. Matching stride for stride, they thundered on toward the woods where Henry VIII had once hunted stags. The wind whipping in Rosanna's face tumbled her hair and tore at the ribbons holding her hat perched so jauntily on her curls. One savage gust separated ribbon from hat and sent it sailing. She twisted, making a grab for it, when she felt the saddle come loose beneath her.

"Chandler! Help me!" Rosanna screamed.

She grabbed desperately, first at the reins, then at the mane, trying to hold on, but the saddle slipped away from Firefly's back. Falling with it, she tried instinctively to leap free. For a heart-stopping moment her boot tangled in the stirrup as she plunged forward. She screamed again as she threw her hands out protectively in front of her. The ground rushing at her and the blur of Firefly's flashing hooves spun before her in a montage of terror. Then there was blackness.

From what seemed like a far distance a steady thudding penetrated into the foggy depths of Rosanna's mind. Dazed, she wanted to sleep more, but something refused to let her slip back into the beckoning darkness. She stirred, slowly moving her head, trying to get away from the bothersome noise, but no matter where she laid her cheek the sound was always there beneath the velvet. Velvet? Yes, that's what she felt. Putting a name to the sensation finally jarred through some of her befuddlement. She stirred again. Velvet covering what? It sounded like a heartbeat, but didn't make any sense.

She heard someone call her name softly. Strong fingers raised her chin. It took an effort, but she was able to bring Chandler's concerned face into focus. A wan smile softened her mouth as she realized he was holding her in his lap. She cuddled her cheek contentedly back down against his dark blue riding jacket and closed her eyes again. The beating of his heart reassured her as she nestled securely into his arms. She was still a bit groggy, but after a time the memory of the toss she'd taken returned clearly to her. She would have loved to remain in his arms forever but knew that was impossible. She moved gingerly, stretching out her legs to see if anything was broken.

"Rosanna, you little fool, you deserve to be spanked for this stunt!" The gentle tone of his voice belied the stern words.

"Have I been out for long?" she whispered. The fog was lifting, but it still took an effort to open her eyes.

"No." He smiled down at her. "You've been like this for only a few minutes."

"What happened?" she asked weakly, making no move at all to free herself from his warm embrace. "I didn't feel Firefly stumble, but suddenly I was heading for a spill and . . . and . . . I just can't remember anything else."

"First tell me how you are feeling. Then, if you're well enough, I'll give you a thundering scold."

His words made her smile. "La," she whined, deliberately mocking Lady Pondesbury, "how could you be so cruel to fuss at me when I'm so obviously unwell? And out here without my parasol! I'm quite overset," she vowed, fluttering her eyelashes.

Chandler's arms tightened deliciously about her. "You

little minx! Now I know you're all right. But there is still a small matter of a frayed cinch."

"The cinch? Oh!" Rosanna cried with an embarrassed flush. "I meant to have that fixed, but, ah, I had other things on my mind that night," she stammered, remembering how Chandler's memory had so disturbed her peace and driven everything from her mind but longing.

"Could that most attractive blush possibly mean you were thinking of me instead of tending to things like cinch mending?"

"What a top lofty presumption, my lord!"

"Indeed? Your eyes hint that your words are a lie." His voice dropped to a husky purr. "Will your lips tell the same story, I wonder?"

Before she could protest, even if she wanted to, Chandler claimed her mouth. The touch was tender, soft, almost teasing. His kiss brushed lightly back and forth over her lips until they were tingling with feeling and yearning for a rougher taking, but her desire was not so easily sated. Instead his mouth nibbled a patch of fire across her cheekbone to the shell of her ear, skillfully heightening her need. His breath was warm as he whispered her name. She tried to turn her face away from the sensations that were driving away all caution, but the hand behind her head wouldn't let her escape. The sweet torture went on and on as a gentle nip on her sensitive earlobe elicited a low moan from her that she had no power to silence.

The fall of her defenses brought a soft chuckle of pleasure from Chandler. His strong arms shifted her slowly away from him. Bemused by her spill and even more by his kiss, Rosanna didn't even react until she felt the coolness of the ground penetrating through her habit. Realizing he had laid her back on the grass, her eyes opened to confront the blazing desire of his gaze. "Chandler, we can't—I mean it's not—"

"Shhh." He placed a finger on the soft curve of her mouth. Leaning over her, he cushioned her head on one arm. His broad chest pushed her deeper into the soft grass as he possessed her mouth again. All the teasing was over as his kiss demanded surrender that she was unable to deny. Rosanna's lips quivered under his when she felt the velvety stroke of his tongue darting tauntingly into the corners of her mouth, then returning to caress over and over the full lower curve until it was throbbing with sensation. Her lips parted hesitantly, allowing a further delightful invasion.

The heaviness of his weight above her sent all sorts of desires flooding through her body. Her hands, instead of pushing him away, found their way around to his back to pull him closer. The kiss plunged deeper as they exchanged pleasure for pleasure. It went on and on, heating Rosanna's blood with a fire she'd never before experienced.

As abruptly as Chandler had taken her, he freed her. Her eyes flew open when she felt him draw away from her. She sat up slowly, a scarlet blush scalding her cheeks. He looked at her, all passion firmly banked. "Hell and damnation, Rosanna, you would tempt a saint! Have we both run mad?"

It must have been madness that had driven her so shamelessly into his arms? Had she no pride? Irritated as much by her surrender as by his blustering, she snapped, "Scarcely a fair question, my lord. You are far from being a saint!"

"Ah, ever the tart tongue. Still I think we both must have bats in our cockloft to do such dallying in so public a place. I admit this glade seems rather secluded, but someone might chance upon us at any moment and your reputation would be in shreds." An engaging grin twisted his mouth which, but a second before, had been deliciously tasting hers. "Must be the amorous ghost of King Henry, still romping about in these woods, that urged us to such doltish behavior."

"Indeed, my lord, it was a most foolish thing!" Rosanna agreed with a pert toss of her head as she struggled to her feet and began brushing off the bits of grass from the velvet of her habit. "I must believe my fall addled my senses."

"And what's my excuse? The springtime nip to the air?" he jested, making light of the situation.

"Your repute would claim you need no excuse."

"Rosanna, I suggest we say no more on the matter," he said, his eyes darkening, "or assuredly we shall either come to dagger drawing or possibly an encore of the moments just past." He ran a hand distractedly through his hair. "I'm not sure which would happen!"

"Dagger drawing seems more our style," she muttered, wishing in her heart the reverse were true. At least he cared enough for propriety to think of her reputation.

Oh, perhaps it was his own reputation he valued. Possibly he feared the amused *on dits* that would fly if anyone knew he had suffered the appalling lapse of good taste to embrace some brown-haired, tart-tongued wench who, as she had heard one old tabby comment, was cast quite in the shade by her sisters.

With a resigned sigh, Rosanna wrapped her dignity about her and determined never to forget herself so wantonly in his arms again. "As you suggest, my lord, nothing more shall be said. Springtime, I agree, is always a treacherous time of the year. We'd best return before Adrian mounts a search party. Where is Firefly? Did he bolt?"

Chandler shook his head. "Your stallion is better trained

than that. When he felt you leave his back, he pulled up immediately. By the time I reined in Bucephalus, he was at your side, nudging you with the utmost concern when you wouldn't wake. But riding him back is quite out of the question. It will take a tackman to mend the cinch. You'll have to ride before me on my saddle until we can get back to the barouche."

His arms felt strong and enticing as they encircled her waist, holding her close as they rode Bucephalus slowly back across the grassy park toward the palace. Though tempted, Rosanna resisted the desire to rest her head against his shoulder. It was distracting enough that, with every jolt, she felt his broad chest rubbing against her back.

CHAPTER
Eight

THE SOCIAL PACE increased as the Season spun down to the last fortnight. So many invitations arrived for musicales, routs, drums, and Venetian breakfasts every day that it was hard for Rosanna and her sisters to choose which to honor with their presence. The Ireland question was also being debated actively in Parliament, and Chandler was often pulled from their side by his duties in the House of Lords. Rosanna had come to learn that he took those duties very seriously.

As she dressed for a masquerade hosted by Lord and Lady Sefton, she couldn't decide if she were glad or not that Chandler was frequently absent. She missed him—his laugh, his banter, his touch. It crossed her mind briefly to wonder if he was deliberately avoiding her, but that made no sense so she pushed away that thought and went back to brushing out her long hair.

Acting on Mr. Brummell's advice never to follow but always to lead, she'd ordered another ruby gown from Monsieur de Montaigne. This one was a silk taffeta with sleeves slashed dashingly in the Spanish manner. A matching domino and mask would cover everything but her gray eyes. Again Brummell's three red roses for her hair arrived as she was stepping out of her lilac-scented bath.

Rosanna was entranced by the Seftons' ballroom, aglitter with hundreds of candles, and was certain she would enjoy her first masquerade. She tried to ignore the feeling that, since Chandler had been delayed by the debates, her enjoyment might be marred.

"My dear, you are in fine looks tonight," Lady Kittering commented to Rosanna. "My nephew ought to be here to fend off the rush that will undoubtedly form, demanding places on your dance card. As for me, rather than get trampled by the herd, I shall go to the card room. Lady Tickbourne made some most odious remarks about my whist playing last time we met. Tonight I plan to give her a sound drubbing!"

As Lady Kittering predicted, Rosanna's card did fill quite rapidly. A waltz was played, and although her partner was an expert dancer, she yearned for Chandler's arms as she was whirled about the room. Out of the corner of her eye, she spotted Edward's unmistakable red hair and was pleased to see him companioning Cecily very attentively. Of course her sister was also flirting with several others as well, but she did seem to be giving Edward some special attention. Perhaps in his own quiet way he could win her over.

For one quadrille she found herself in the same set with their Almack's patroness. Even her jeweled domino couldn't disguise Lady Jersey's animated personality. Noted for her incessant chatter, she had earned the nickname "silence." "I trust, Lady Wythe," the patroness commented when she and Rosanna passed during the dance, "that you received your invitation to our theater party and midnight breakfast."

"Indeed." Rosanna nodded as the pattern brought them back together. "We will be honored to attend. Rumor has it you've snared a most unusual guest."

"How vexing! I meant for that to be a surprise, but I suppose there are few secrets during the Season." She laughed lightly. "Let us sit the next dance out so I can tell you all about it."

Lady Jersey was fanning herself vigorously when Rosanna joined her. "I sent my partner off after some ices," Rosanna commented, settling down in the chair next to the older woman. "Is it true that Basil Dudley will attend your breakfast?"

"Yes. I don't mean to brag, but it is quite a plume in my bonnet to secure the attendance of the greatest living Shakespearean actor. Not only that, they say he is the very devil with the ladies! Doesn't that sound delicious? Where was I? Oh yes, we shall attend Dudley's performance of *Hamlet* at Vauxhall Gardens, then return for the rout. Lord Jersey has secured a large box for us, so why don't you and your sisters join us? That will make a cozy group." Her eyes sparkled mischievously. "It would appear that I should also tender an invitation to Hartwick's friend Edward Maitland, as well as that neighbor of yours from Somerset, Adrian Cameron."

Rosanna laughed at Lady Jersey's perceptive noting of who was courting whom in the *ton*. "And for you, Lady Wythe, it shall be—"

"It shall be no one!" Rosanna interrupted insistently. "I'm not dangling for a husband. Remember I had one once. It didn't suit."

"We shall see." Lady Jersey smiled mysteriously.

The evening was winding down to the moment of unmasking when Rosanna again found herself at Lady Jersey's side. "Why aren't you waltzing, Lady Wythe? Surely those slippers of yours aren't tired of the whirl."

"No. Actually Lady Tickbourne's son asked me to stand up with him, but I pleaded fatigue."

"Wise indeed. His feet would do better stomping dirt clods than stepping on ladies' toes."

Suddenly a deep voice inquired, "Perhaps the scarlet domino would accept me as a substitute?"

A mask of royal blue covered half his face, but there was no doubt who owned that rich tone or that breadth of shoulders. "It appears you have a mysterious gallant, Lady Domino in Scarlet," commented Lady Jersey, delighting in the match making. "Shall I perform the introductions so that you can waltz?"

"No introductions are needed on a night of the masquerade. Besides," Chandler vowed, wrapping a strong arm around Rosanna's waist and pulling her toward the dance floor, "this waltz is bespoke." He added under his breath, "Even if the lady again chooses to wear someone else's flowers in her hair."

It was fun to continue the game and flirt outrageously as they whirled about the floor. The mask hiding Rosanna's face made it easy to play the coquette. "Indeed, sir, this waltz was bespoke, but by Thomas Tickbourne. There must be some misunderstanding."

"The only misunderstanding is on your part, milady, for deeding over one of my waltzes."

"Yours indeed! Fiddle! You were nowhere about earlier to claim them. Was I to sit in the dowager row most primly until you decided to appear? Would a scarlet domino be so poor spirited? It's very unlikely, I assure you!"

The arm about her waist pulled her closer. "You might have waited for your blue domino. The night couldn't pass without the claiming of at least one waltz."

"And how was I to know the blue domino would even appear? The only message I received this evening came with my roses."

"Roses?" he commented, his hand leaving her waist

to pluck the offending blossoms from her curls. Over her protests, they fell one by one to the floor. "You must be mistaken. I see no roses, so there couldn't have been a message. I vow the spirited scarlet domino has a spirited imagination as well, but that is a small penalty to pay for holding such an excellent dancer in my arms."

Rosanna longed to ask him if her dancing skill was the only reason he wished her in his arms, but the words froze in her throat. Instead she inquired, "Are you attending Lady Jersey's theater party, or will the debates demand your time again?"

Silence. She peeked up at him, wondering why he suddenly looked a bit like a little boy caught stealing apples. "Ah," he admitted after a long pause, "I fear I have a previous appointment that night, but I should see you at the rout following the play." His arm tightened possessively about her waist. "And no hedging this time. All the waltzes are mine! I would detest fighting a duel with that nodcock Tickbourne merely to claim the waltzes you've already given me."

"When did I give you all my waltzes? I don't recall doing any such thing."

With an arrogant wave of his hand, Chandler dismissed her denial as he asked, "Have you another ruby gown on order for the evening?"

"Yes, one of scarlet with a silver underdress. But why do you ask?"

"Good! You can expect the flowers for the rout to come from me! As the guardian for your sisters, I don't feel the elder sister should set a bad example by sporting a mysterious gallant's tribute in her hair. It is most improper."

Before Rosanna had a chance to retort to this idiocy, the music ended their waltz. Chandler dropped his arm

slowly from her waist as a drum roll signaled the unmasking. His touch was gentle as it brushed her cheeks,
then moved to the strings of her mask. It fell into his
hands, but he made no move to take off his own.

Rosanna could see his blue eyes glittering behind the
slits in his mask. She lifted her hand hesitantly toward
him. Her fingers trembled as they became tangled in his
sun-streaked hair, searching for the ties. He seemed to
delight in the unsettling effect he was having on her.
Smiling, he reached up, closed his hand over hers, and
guided it to the knot. When the domino came loose she
tried to pull free from the disturbing warmth, but her
hand remained imprisoned alluringly as he carried it to
his mouth for a lingering kiss. It was the perfect end to
a lovely masquerade.

The mild evening air caressed Rosanna's shoulders as
she followed Lucinda and Cecily into Vauxhall Gardens
later that week to view Basil Dudley's performance of
Hamlet. Lady Kittering, fatigued by all the gadabouting,
had opted to remain home. The gardens were lit with
scores of lanterns glimmering in the overhead branches
that lent a magical quality to the darkening sky. Hawkers
of everything from flowers, to oatcakes, to palm reading,
vied for the attention and coins of passersby, and it reminded Rosanna of the country fairs they had in Somerset
after every harvest.

As she and her sisters strolled slowly along the path
toward the theater area, as if by mere chance Edward
and Adrian appeared out of the crowd to escort the twins.
Rosanna smiled, knowing there was nothing at all casual
about the meeting. Then her smile faded as she watched
Cecily laughing flirtatiously with Edward while Adrian
and Lucinda wandered off, talking quitely together, lost
in their world of growing love. Rosanna was glad her

sisters had attracted two such fine companions, yet she couldn't still a feeling of loneliness as she watched them. Was this the future for her, a future alone? Thinking of Chandler, she touched the three red roses that he had sent which were nestled in her hair. Hoping the appointment he had mentioned earlier—which she had assumed had to do with government matters—would be over soon and he might appear unexpectedly, as he had at the Sefton masquerade, she kept scanning the crowd as they moved on toward the Jerseys' theater box. As the lanterns flickered out for the beginning of the play, Rosanna's wish remained unanswered.

Basil Dudley enthralled the audience with his tragic portrayel of Hamlet. Generous applause rang out from the usually bored *ton* as the lights came up after the first act. Rosanna's clapping ceased abruptly when she glanced across the floor and saw Chandler dancing close attendance on Elvinia in her box. The other woman's hand curled possessively around his arm as she cooed at him, most sickeningly it seemed to Rosanna.

Lady Jersey's sharp eyes apparently missed none of the exchange either. A mischievous smile was playing on her lips as she tapped Rosanna on the knee with her ever-present fan. "An equal flirtation would better serve, milady," Lady Jersey said. "To let a man unsettle you by his attentions to another woman is fatal! Have no fear, we'll contrive something." Ignoring Rosanna's protests, Lady Jersey leaned over and whispered a few words to her husband, who grinned and immediately left the box.

Realizing that the society matron's advice was good, Rosanna forced a bright smile to her lips as she listened to their group's comments on the first act. She didn't venture another glance at Chandler and the clinging Elvinia.

Cecily was especially animated, raving over Dudley's

performance. "Just imagine how wonderful it would be to play Ophelia to his Hamlet." She sighed. "I would scarce have to act to pretend he holds my heart! Edward, didn't you think he was simply marvelous?"

"Not particularly." Edward shrugged, his frown clearly marking his displeasure as Cecily's raptures of Dudley continued.

It was Rosanna's turn to sigh. Obviously Cecily was once more enamored. Blast it all! It would be harder than ever for her to see Edward's worth with the romantic image of the actor hanging between them.

She was yanked out of her musing when Brummell and two other prominent *tonnish* bachelors entered their box, followed by a smiling Lord Jersey. The three younger men each carried a huge bunch of red roses, which they presented with a most formal flourish before drawing up chairs to surround Rosanna with admiring attention. Lady Jersey, obviously pleased with her husband's conspiring, rewarded him with a kiss.

Rosanna buried her face in the scented flowers, then sneaked a quick peek at Chandler and was delighted to see that things were not going smoothly in the box across the way. The mulish set to Elvinia's mouth and Chandler's thunderous frown told most plainly that they'd noticed Rosanna's cortege of admirers and didn't approve. She hoped Chandler would connect the bouquets of red roses with the flowers Brummell had sent. It would do him good to wonder if she had more than one mysterious gallant! Smiling flirtatiously at Brummell, Rosanna let her fingers play leisurely on his coat sleeve as she returned banter for banter before the lights dimmed for the last act.

In the box across from Rosanna things were, indeed, not going smoothly. Elvinia waited until the actors had started their lines, then pouted, "La, you are paying more attention to that creature over there than you are to me. Can't you see that Lady Wythe has more admirers now than she can use. Why must you ogle her as well?"

"I wished merely to see who was paying such extravagant court to her," Chandler explained calmly, trying to keep his voice from betraying his irritation.

"Why should you care? She's not your ward. I beg you to remember she is a widow. She can take care of herself!"

Obviously realizing her tactics were failing, Elvinia softened her voice to a seductive purr. She let her fingers brush suggestively against Chandler's thigh as she reached for his hand. "I declare, why are we spatting over that foolish woman? Tonight is too beautiful to spoil with a silly argument."

Chandler pulled his hand away from her possessive grasp. "The play is also being spoiled. Ophelia's death scene is coming up. I shouldn't want to miss that."

Elvinia stamped her foot. "She'll die again tomorrow night. You can come and see it then. I must talk to you! We haven't had a private moment together in an age." She put her hand back on his arm. "Something has happened. Something I must tell you that concerns us."

Chandler looked down at her with an exasperated sigh. The dim lights from the stage cast softly romantic shadows on her face, a face with admittedly few rivals. His eyes swept over her, but he felt nothing. "What happened?" he asked, not really caring a jot.

Boredom dulled his voice, but apparently Elvinia didn't notice as she stroked his sleeve. "Neville Tweedsmuir has asked me to marry him."

"Congratulations."

"Congratulations! Is that all you have to say?" she shrilled, digging her fingernails into his sleeve.

"No, I can also ask you to please let go of my coat. I don't wish to arrive at the Jerseys' ball with a mangled sleeve."

"Don't you care that I might marry another man?"

"Your screech is beginning to draw attention to us. Do you wish to share our discussion with the whole *ton?*"

"I don't care! You have to do—"

"No, Elvinia, I don't have to *do* anything. You might as well save your ammunition for poor Neville. I've had traps laid by the best, and I'm not going to fall into yours. I realize you're trying to force me to come up to scratch by throwing Tweedsmuir's offer in my face, but it's not going to work. I'm not interested. I'm interested only in seeing the end of this play." When he fell silent Elvinia gave an angry sniff and flounced out of the box.

After the play was over Rosanna deliberately ignored Chandler's presence across the way. With a flirtatious smile, she handed the bouquets to one of her gallants and, linking arms with the other two, left the theater for the Jerseys' ball.

Lady Jersey, renowned as much for her unique parties as for her ceaseless matchmaking, had decorated the ballroom at their mansion like a Bedouin encampment with iced champagne in one striped silk tent, food in another, a band concealed in the third. There was even an artfully placed fence enclosing two baaing sheep and a goat.

Brummell, still at Rosanna's side, looked at the lowly animals and wrinkled a fastidious nose. "Sally's freaks become more bizarre with each passing year. I trust she bathed those creatures. Can you imagine the tumult if they should escape? There would be women screaming and fainting all over the place."

Rosanna laughed. "You know you delight in her originality. After all, you were the one who advised me not to follow the crowd, but be daring."

"What you say is true, milady, but being daring most assuredly does not mean dragging dumb beasts into the ballroom."

"I'm afraid I must agree with that. Having lived in the country, I know sheep are incredibly lacking in sense. And I will be lacking in sense as well if I forget to thank you for sitting in my pocket during the play. It was most kind."

"Your as odd a creature as that goat there if you think I and the others were merely being kind," Brummell insisted. "It's past time you realized that you're a lovely, intriguing woman who men delight in being beside. Are the men in Somerset such dolts that nobody has made you truly see yourself?"

"Perhaps I never gave them or myself a chance," Rosanna admitted, remembering how she'd buried herself at Millbourne Hall.

"Then I'm honored to able to enlighten you on the subject. Now, on to another important matter. What have you and our little French friend designed for the fireworks in honor of the Duke of Wellington? I thought perhaps—"

"Could the discussion of fashion wait?" Lady Jersey interrupted. "I have a delightful surprise for Lady Wythe." She moved to one side and Rosanna was shocked to come face to face with Sir Wilbert. "I have found a relation of yours."

"He is no relation of mine!" she stated, with a sharp snap of her fan. "The relationship, as distasteful as it is, is on my late husband's side. I have no wish to be rude after all of your kindness, Lady Jersey, but even to please you I shall not recognize this . . . this . . . person." Without another word, she turned her back.

Lady Jersey held no book with toadying interlopers. "Oh, do go away, Sir Wilbert." She waved her fan at him. "Obviously you are most unwelcome. We shan't eject you from the party, but if Lady Wythe objects to your presence, you will be scratched from all future guest lists."

"I warn you, Lady Wythe, one day you'll pay well for your top-lofty airs!" Sir Wilbert threatened as he stomped off.

"What an incredibly boorish man! But pay him no heed," Lady Jersey advised. "His type is always big on words, but too cowardly to take action." She laid a hand on Rosanna's rigid arm. "My friend, I must ask for your forgiveness. He gave Lord Jersey to understand he was a close connection of yours. I thought you'd be pleased to have a relation invited to the rout. Truly I am sorry. I won't make such a mistake again."

Rosanna turned to her and managed a wan smile. "I must explain."

"No explanations are necessary," Brummell insisted. "Your taste is impeccable. Your reasons for refusing the introduction are, no doubt, excellent. The next time, if he dares encroach, we shall all cut him dead."

"Indeed we shall," Lady Jersey agreed. "Come, let us inspect the darling sheep and then visit the food tent."

"Lady Jersey, I have several words to say to you about this preposterous livestock," Brummell fussed as they started across the floor.

An uneasy feeling prickled up Rosanna's spine as she followed. Glancing back over her shoulder, she saw Sir Wilbert watching them. It was hard to believe a round, pudgy face could form into such a menacing glower. He was obviously livid that she'd repudiated him in public.

She wondered nervously if Lady Jersey was right. Was his warning just a bluff or would he seek revenge?

Sir Wilbert's small eyes squinted over the ballroom and she saw an ugly smile curl his fat lips. She followed the direction of his gaze, but saw only Basil Dudley holding court at the far end of the ballroom. She shrugged as Wilbert started toward the actor. She was probably being fanciful. Granted, Sir Wilbert was furious at the moment but he couldn't do anything to harm her or the twins, could he?

She looked across the floor again and saw Sir Wilbert throw a guilty glance over his shoulder. Perhaps he was up to some mischief. As unobtrusively as possible she began to edge nearer in hopes of hearing his conversation with Dudley.

Sets for a country dance were beginning to form as Rosanna carefully approached the group surrounding the actor. She didn't want Sir Wilbert to see her, so she stayed on the far side of the milling dancers. The first words of their conversation helped reassure her that Wilbert wasn't up to any harm.

"Pray stand aside and allow my dear friend, Sir Wilbert, to join us," she heard the actor order with a sweep of his arm as Sir Wilbert approached. "Have you tasted of this most exceptional champagne? You fellow, there," he called dramatically to a passing waiter, "bring that tray of glasses this way. My friend's throat is parched."

Basil grabbed a glass and handed it to Wilbert. "Drink up! The stuff sure beats the slop they draw at that inn where we lodge."

Rosanna shook her head. Their chatter seemed innocent enough. No doubt she was being ridiculously suspicious to suspect Sir Wilbert of anything other than wanting to bask in the reflected glory of his acting friend.

Feeling a bit foolish, she was about to move away when she heard Wilbert interrupt the fawning compliments the people around them were heaping on Basil's performance.

"Dudley," Sir Wilbert's grating voice carried to her, "I've seen someone you should meet. Perhaps I can manage an introduction for you. I assure you, you'll be most interested," he promised, drawing the actor away from his circle of admirers.

"Why should I be interested in some dreary acquaintance of yours?" Dudley drawled when they were standing alone.

"I know your taste runs to innocents. Believe me, meeting this very tempting piece will be well worth your while."

Rosanna noted the skeptical slant to the actor's eyes as he commented, "In all the time we've lodged at the same inn, you've never before thrown a chit my way. Why now?"

"Let's just say I'd like to do you a favor and, just perhaps, the favor will be returned."

Rosanna didn't like Sir Wilbert's mysterious chuckle. Could he be talking about her sisters? Rosanna wondered. No, that was nonsense. They were simply two men exchanging some typically ribald chatter. Chandler had said she had a spirited imagination. Well, it was certainly being unnecessarily active where Sir Wilbert was concerned. Lady Jersey was right. People like Giles's cousin threatened but were too cowardly to act.

Yet for all the commonsense advice she was giving herself, Rosanna couldn't stop a quiver of doubt. She glanced around the ballroom and was relieved to see Cecily in a set with Edward and Lucinda entering the food tent on Adrian's arm. They were well protected.

Still, it wouldn't hurt to remind them of Dudley's reputation, she decided as the orchestra started the rousing music for the dance. The two men continued talking, but Rosanna couldn't hear what they were saying. It looked as though Wilbert was attempting to convince Dudley of something. She was trying to decide if she dared slip closer when Lady Jersey approached.

"I thought you were going to join us in sampling the food," Lady Jersey observed, reaching Rosanna's side. "I looked around and you were gone. Are you feeling well? I noticed your frown as I was walking over."

Rosanna shrugged away he uneasy feeling about Sir Wilbert. "I confess I do have a slight migraine. Maybe it's the loud music."

"Ah, I have the cure for that. Come with me to the conservatory," Lady Jersey suggested, taking Rosanna's arm. "Some new orchids just arrived from South America. Lord Jersey is quite proud of them."

Rosanna hesitated a moment, throwing one last glance at the two men she'd been watching, but a tug on her arm recalled her attention. Reluctantly she agreed to see Lord Jersey's orchids.

Chandler stood not far away, pretending to listen to the trivial comments of a young peer beside him. His gaze wandered idly about the room, then rested on Rosanna's back as she disappeared into the conservatory. He frowned, wondering which of her admirers could have enticed her in there, then forced himself to look away. Who Rosanna amused herself with was truly no concern of his. His time would be better spent watching out for his young wards.

He quickly located Lucinda and Adrian filling their plates in the food tent. Chandler couldn't understand what Lucinda saw in the viscount, but was pleased that at least Adrian was interested in her and not Rosanna. Scowling again at the thought of the twins' older sister, Chandler continued looking for Cecily.

She was not far from him, and Chandler's expression darkened when he saw that her companion was the dandified actor Basil Dudley, and that the actor was in the process of kissing Cecily's hand. Without apologizing to the peer babbling beside him, Chandler strode forcefully across the room, intent on collaring the actor and delivering Cecily the scold of her life. He was not halfway there when he met Rosanna emerging from the conservatory.

"I see sneaking kisses runs in the Millbourne family!" he snapped. "Conservatories are always so convenient for such dallying, aren't they? Which of your rose-giving gallants did you favor with your affections this time? Or perhaps I shouldn't ask. Obviously your tryst among the flowers didn't go smashingly or you wouldn't have left your swain amid the potted plants!"

"Who I left amid the plants—or, to be more precise, orchids—was Lady Jersey. Now if you will let me pass, I wish to find my sisters! The air has suddenly become a bit unpleasant in this part of the ballroom." Rosanna turned to go, but tossed a question over her shoulder. "Oh, by the by, how was your 'appointment' with dear Lady Pondesbury? Government business is such a bore, isn't it?"

Chandler raised his voice. "I never said my appointment concerned a Parliamentary matter, but it might as well have. To be completely honest, my appointment, as you call it, was about as amorous as your stroll to view the orchids—and certainly not as enjoyable."

That confession halted Rosanna in mid-step. She

glanced back at him. "A lover's spat, my lord? How distressing!"

"I can tell you shall cry buckets over my problems." Chandler grinned, then quickly became more serious. "All this delightful sparring doesn't get us to the truly distressing problem, which provoked my original charge."

Rosanna read the concern on his face and returned quickly to his side. "Chandler, what is it? Has Lady Kittering been taken ill? I knew she was tired. I never should have left her tonight. We must—"

He possessed himself of her hands. "Rosanna, your words tumble over each other like stones in an avalanche. Lady Kittering is fine. It's Cecily I'm concerned about. Whilst you were in the conservatory, Cecily was here carrying on a hand-kissing flirtation with that scoundrel Basil Dudley. His reputation as a favorer of young misses is common gossip."

"Hand-kissing with an actor!" Rosanna gasped. "Are you sure? When I left she was dancing with your friend Edward. I felt her safe enough with him."

"It may be Dudley who's unsafe, judging from the murderous expression I saw on Edward's face as he watched the same scene I did."

Her suspicions of Wilbert returned. "Who introduced them? Do you know?"

"I have no idea. All I saw was that scoundrel nuzzling her hand."

"Rest assured, Chandler, I shall talk to her about this nonsense!"

CHAPTER
Nine

ROSANNA WASTED NO time the next morning in delivering a scold to Cecily. Her sister was sipping hot chocolate when Rosanna entered her bedchamber. "Oh, Rosanna, wasn't last night smashing fun?" Cecily beamed. "I have so much to tell you. The most exciting thing happened. I met Basil Dudley and he—"

"Yes, I know." Rosanna's stern tone forced the happy smile from Cecily's face. "I also know you allowed him to kiss your hand."

"Oh, phoo!" Cecily pouted. "What's wrong with that? I've seen our guardian kissing your hand in public, and you don't object."

"It is hardly the same thing!"

"Why not?"

Rosanna saw the mulish set to her sister's mouth and frowned. Cecily simply refused to understand that her flirting could lead her into trouble that she might not be able to handle. She walked over and sat on the bed next to her younger sister. She patiently tried to explain again. "Please believe me, Cecily, I'm only concerned about you. I won't go into details, but Basil Dudley has a very foul reputation, especially where young, innocent misses are concerned."

"It couldn't be too bad, or Lady Jersey would never have invited him to her party."

Rosanna sighed. "I know it's difficult to understand, but Lady Jersey invited that actor as a conversation piece—a novelty—to entertain her guests. To put it quite bluntly, he was part of the evening's amusement."

When Cecily didn't answer, Rosanna insisted, "I want you to promise you'll be more careful in the future. Flirting with a man of Dudley's stamp is vastly different from making young Bromley stutter. It's also more dangerous!"

"Dangerous? Really, Rosanna, aren't you being just a bit dramatic? All the man did was kiss my hand."

"If it takes being dramatic to make you listen and be sensible, then that's what I'll do! Basil Dudley isn't to be trusted. Will you please heed my advice?"

"Oh, very well," Cecily conceded with a shrug. "Even though his chatter is the most entertaining I've encountered in ever so long, if you insist, I'll behave like a proper miss."

"I *do* insist." Rosanna studied her sister as she casually sipped her morning chocolate. Even though Cecily had agreed, Rosanna didn't like the excited glitter that still sparkled deep in her sister's blue eyes. Perhaps she was being fanciful, but she suspected something was afoot. If only Cecily were as sensible as Lucinda and would listen to her warning, but Rosanna wasn't sure she would. She just hoped she'd be on hand if Cecily fell into trouble.

She leaned over and gave her younger sister a hug. "You know I hate to fuss at you, but I feel responsible. By the way, who introduced you to the actor?"

"I don't know." Cecily patted a yawn. "Some man. I was too excited about meeting Mr. Dudley to pay much attention to him."

Rosanna let the matter drop. "Please remember what I said and be careful. Now hurry with that drink and get dressed. We must visit Bond Street today and shop for something to wear to the fireworks display."

After Rosanna was attired in a morning dress of deepest primrose, she took the book of Molière's plays she'd finished back to the library. Chandler was at his desk writing notes for another speech. Rosanna's concern for Cecily must have shown on her expression because Chandler laid down his quill pen immediately and observed, "From that frown, I'd judge Molière's humor left you untouched..I've always found him quite witty."

Rosanna forced a smile. Regardless of her father's will, she felt that Cecily was her responsibility, not Chandler's, and she wasn't going to burden him with her problems. Besides, maybe she'd just imagined that sparkle in Cecily's eyes.

"Oh, I agree." She nodded before replacing the book in its place on the shelf. "Witty is one word for his style."

"Your most attractive blush indicates that perhaps bawdy would be a better description."

She glanced at him, then away. Why did he smile in such a beguiling manner? The warmth in his gaze fired an answering flutter of desire in her body. It was no use pretending that his smile didn't ignite dangerously alluring feelings within her. Blast the man! Before entering the room Rosanna had only been concerned about Cecily. But no doubt she herself was the one who'd better take care!

Refusing to let him see how he'd stirred her emotions, Rosanna bravely pulled her glance back to meet his. "Molière was writing about the court of Louis XIV. You could hardly expect him to resist poking fun at all the lecherous nonsense that was going on there."

Before Chandler could comment, she changed the topic. "Do you plan to accompany us to the fireworks

Saturday? Word has it that it will be quite a spectacular conclusion to the Season."

"I can escort you there, but then, I'm afraid, I'll have to leave and—"

"Oh, let me guess," Rosanna interrupted with a pert toss of her head. "I surmise you have another appointment, like the 'appointment' whose box you shared at Vauxhall Gardens."

Chandler pushed back his chair and stood up. In a few powerful strides he was towering over her. "Rosanna, unless you want fireworks exploding in here, you will stop uttering such nonsense. Besides, I'm surprised you even noticed I had a companion that evening. You seemed completely enthralled with the host of admirers who were surrounding you with red roses."

Rosanna hoped her smile looked vastly more serene than she felt. "The gentlemen were kind, weren't they? No doubt I can find someone to escort us once we arrive at St. James's Park. I know you wouldn't want to keep your 'appointment' waiting."

"No, I wouldn't! From experience, I know what an explosive temper he has if anyone is late."

"He?" Her eyes widened in surprise.

"You heard me correctly. I can't stay with you in the park because the Duke of Wellington has asked me and some of the other officers who fought beside him in the Peninsula to share the reviewing stand with him. It's an honor I'm very pleased to accept. Although, I admit, after fencing words with you, I'm sure the fireworks display itself will seem quite dull."

"I believe I'll take that as a compliment." It pleased Rosanna that she wasn't the only one affected by their moments together.

"I'm not sure I meant it that way." He laughed, shaking his head. "I've never met a woman quite like you,

Rosanna. You discuss history and estate management one moment, and openly court the attentions of a confirmed flirt like Brummell the next." His eyes darkened to deep sapphire. "You're an interesting challenge, and I've always been intrigued by a challenge," he murmured with a velvety softness that made her heart pound.

The air between them tingled with an intensity of feeling that startled Rosanna. Did he feel it, too, or was she only imagining the disquieting sensations? For an instant, she thought Chandler was about to reach for her, but he turned instead and went back to his desk. The moment was gone.

He dismissed her almost gruffly. "My aunt said a shopping outing was in your plans for today. I know the merchants in Bond Street are eagerly awaiting your business. I'll see you later."

Confused by his abrupt shift in mood, Rosanna slowly left the room. The rest of the week was so busy she didn't have time to reflect on the matter.

The shopping trip had been a success, Rosanna decided Saturday as she pivoted in front of the cheval glass. She and Monsieur de Montaigne had discussed the fact that everyone would expect her to appear in a ruby-red gown like the ones she'd worn before, so they'd decided to do something different. He'd brought out a length of raw silk fabric dyed to a deep sapphire. The color reminded Rosanna forcefully of Chandler's eyes when he'd gazed down at her earlier that morning. She knew he would somehow seem closer if she wore this particular shade of blue. She had refused to consider any other piece of silk.

Rosanna was delighted with the walking dress the Frenchman had created, but she wished he hadn't scooped the neckline quite so low and drawn special attention to the soft swell of her breasts by adding pale blue lacings. She momentarily considered draping a lace fichu about her shoulders to conceal the provocative lines of the bodice, then lifted her chin boldly. If Lady Pondesbury could sport such daring gowns, so could she! The *ton* was large enough to accommodate two dashing widows. She told herself her decision was a direct challenge to the other woman. Her heart knew, in truth, she hoped to kindle Chandler's interest by her daring.

Rosanna was giving the finishing strokes to her long hair when Cecily and Lucinda entered her bedchamber. "I do believe it's my turn to scold, dear sister," Cecily teased lightly. "You fuss at me for flirting with Basil Dudley, then have the nerve to wear a gown like that! You're flirting openly without saying a word."

"Oh, don't listen to her chatter, Rosanna," Lucinda told her. "I think you look lovely. Cecily's merely jealous because we always have to wear these insipid pastel colors."

"That's the only advantage to being most permanently on the shelf—I can wear what I wish. Besides," Rosanna added, looking at her sisters with pride, "with you two about, no one will bother a glance at me."

But as they came down the sweeping staircase, Chandler didn't even look at the twins. His gaze raked caressingly down Rosanna's body, then returned for lingering moments on the rounded thrust of her breasts. The fire in his eyes warmed her blood as if he'd actually touched her. Her breath came quicker as a response stirred in her body.

Lady Kittering called him to order with a loud rap of her cane. "Stop making sheep's eyes at Rosanna, dear boy, and call for that carriage. I want to get to St. James's Park early enough to have a word or two with Wellington. He always was a favorite of mine."

Dusk was settling gently down on the park as they arrived. As Rosanna walked beside Chandler along the garden paths, the shadows added to the romantic atmosphere. The twins' chatter faded farther and farther away as she savored the magic of the night and the beguiling pull of Chandler's nearness. He seemed to sense it too, as he lifted her hand and tucked it firmly into the crook of his arm. His touch remained, caressing over her fingertips, the back of her hand, the sensitive area of her wrist. An intimate smile curved his firm lips as he gazed down at her. Their steps slowed, both unwilling to hurry toward the reviewing stand where they would have to part.

All too soon, the gravel path wound to a halt in front of the gaily decorated stand. The Iron Duke's bellowing voice ripped through the sensuous web of feeling that had surrounded them. "Ho, Hartwick, glad you've arrived." Wellington gestured disdainfully toward several of England's most famous admirals, who were sharing the seats with him. "Been lecturing these sailors here on how a real battle is fought. Come tell them how you earned that court-martial at Talavera!"

With obvious reluctance Chandler dropped Rosanna's hand. "I'll try to escape the reminiscences after the fireworks are over and come and find you," he murmured. "At least I don't have to worry about a swarm of admirers casting bouquets of red roses at you this evening while I'm occupied refighting the Peninsula Wars. Red roses would hardly go with that gown."

"True, but surely my admirers, as you call them, can't fail to see how lovely a spray of white heather would accent this color."

From the hard glitter in Chandler's eyes, she knew he was about to retort to her pert teasing when Wellington's gruff voice intervened. "Hartwick, you can dally

with that most attractive lady later. I need your help now
to convince these bilgewater captains how much more
complex military strategy is on land."

Lady Kittering remained with Chandler as Rosanna
and her sisters strolled on through the darkening park.
Lanterns strung from the branches guided them toward
the large open area where spectators were gathering for
the display. Adrian apparently had been watching for
them because, before they even left the pathway, Rosanna saw him hurrying to their side. Claiming he wanted
to share some news from Somerset with Lucinda, he
detached her from the group. It was a very shallow pretext
and the pair lagged behind noticeably, but Rosanna ap-
proved of Adrian's suit and didn't want to throw a spoke
in his plans.

The next meeting, however, didn't please her. At a
bend in the path, she and Cecily encountered Basil Dudley. He tried to pretend it was merely a chance meeting,
but Rosanna had her doubts on that score. Was this why
Cecily's eyes had sparkled so mischievously the other
morning? Had her sister and the actor planned this rendezvous?

The actor didn't try to conceal his vexation when
Rosanna refused to let him draw Cecily far from her side.
She didn't care. Her only concession was to withdraw a
few steps, but she remained visible and clearly attentive
to their dalliance. Keeping one ear attuned to their flirtatious banter, she glanced over the assembled *tonnish*
crowd, looking hopefully for a flash of red hair. If only
Edward Maitland would appear, but she didn't spot him.

Rosanna's fingers tightened even more around the
strings of her reticule when Dudley heartily welcomed a
man approaching them. It was Sir Wilbert, and Rosanna
deliberately withdrew several paces from the threesome,
not wanting any further contact with Giles's cousin. She

noticed that he was sporting the dreadful puce waistcoat, as well as a silver-headed walking stick. The uneasy feeling she always got around him prickled along her nerves again. She didn't like the man and liked even less the unexplained smirk curling his fat lips as his glance slid over Cecily. Rosanna moved instinctively nearer so she could hear every word spoken.

Wilbert greeted Cecily, then added, "I'm pleased to see you are getting along so well with my dear friend Basil. It was obviously an inspiration that led me to introduce the two of you, for I have never seen a more lovely or better-matched couple."

Cecily giggled in response, covering Rosanna's unconscious gasp. *Wilbert* had introduced Basil Dudley to Cecily! Now she was certain the actor was up to no good with her sister.

Sir Wilbert and the actor exchanged a few more pleasantries then Wilbert pulled a folded paper from inside his coat. He handed it to the actor and, although Cecily couldn't, Rosanna could see the sly wink Wilbert gave Dudley. "This came after you left," Sir Wilbert explained "I thought you'd be interested in the invitation."

Basil opened the sheet, quickly scanned the message, then shoved it hastily into a pocket. "Ah, yes, I am interested. It sounds like a most enjoyable way to while away the evening, doesn't it?"

Sir Wilbert's only answer was another smirk. To Rosanna's relief, he soon took his leave and Cecily was once again alone with Basil. As they continued on their way, the actor tossed more flowery compliments in Cecily's direction. At one point, he pulled his handkerchief from a pocket to aid his dramatic gestures, and a piece of paper fluttered to the ground behind him.

Rosanna quickened her step until she was standing next to the dropped paper. Pretending to have a stone in her kid slipper, she knelt and concealed the note in her reticule. She didn't trust Basil and, unfortunately, she couldn't trust Cecily's good judgment either.

As the lamplighters began to douse the lanterns for the start of the fireworks, they all moved toward the open area for a clear view of the colorful sprays of light that were beginning to explode over their heads. The fireworks mimicked a great battle scene as clusters of red sparks shot from one side of the park and crashed into glittering blue and gold flashes that came from the other side. The explosions even sounded liked cannon fire as flaming balls exploded into a cascade of shooting lights. The finale to the performance was a huge Union Jack done in a blaze of red, white, and blue fireworks, accompanied by the band playing a rousing "God Save the King," in honor of the Regent, who was sitting prominently at Wellington's side.

When the relit lanterns flooded the area with soft light, Rosanna looked around for her sisters. Adrian and Lucinda were standing a short distance away, but Cecily was nowhere to be seen. Worried, Rosanna wandered through the crowd searching for her irresponsible sister.

"Lady Wythe, might I have a word with you?" a man's voice called.

Rosanna turned eagerly, but it was only Edward Maitland. Her disappointment must have shown because his smile disappeared. "I don't wish to seem overly bold, but something is obviously wrong. I'd like to offer my help."

The last thing Rosanna wanted was to have the tale of Cecily's disappearance spread through the *ton*, but she knew she could trust Edward to be discreet. With effort, she kept her voice calm. "I hesitate to believe anything is truly wrong, Mr. Maitland, but I would appreciate your help in searching for Cecily. She seems to have wandered off during the fireworks display. It was dark and I'm sure we've just been accidently separated, yet in this crowd I do worry."

Frowning with concern, Edward asked where Rosanna had last seen Cecily, then started off at a rapid trot to begin his search. When Rosanna turned in the opposite direction, her reticule bumped against her leg. The crackle of paper reminded her of the invitation Basil had dropped. Of course, why hadn't she thought of that before? Probably thinking it was terribly romantic, Cecily might have stolen away to attend some party. Rosanna pulled the invitation quickly out of her purse. By the light of a flickering lantern she read:

> Dudley, another lively romp is scheduled for to-
> night at 1806 Tamberly. Bring a "lady friend" or
> come by yourself. I've decanted a bottle of your
> favorite wine for you so don't disappoint me
>
> Mavis

Rosanna's first thought was to find Chandler. But no, Cecily was her responsibility. She had the address, so she could drag her sister out of the party before any harm was done. Rosanna was near the edge of the park when she made her impulsive decision. A number of hackney cabs, waiting for passengers to leave the fireworks display, were lined up in the Mall. She had no trouble finding a driver who would take her to Tamberly Street. She noticed the strange look he gave her when she told him the address, but was too worried about Cecily to wonder about it.

Having made his excuses to Wellington, Chandler scanned the crowd and caught sight of a friend. "Edward, where are you marching off to," he called. "You look like you're ready to do battle. What's wrong?"

"Cecily's missing. Lady Wythe asked me to search for her. Hell and damnation, if my horse hadn't thrown a shoe, I wouldn't have been late! Where can she be? If anything has happened to her, I don't... We must find her!"

Fear echoed through his voice, telling Chandler more eloquently than any words how deeply in love his friend had fallen. "Buck up! She's here someplace. Did you look by those rose bushes? Perhaps she wandered over there to enjoy the flowers."

Although Chandler was several inches taller than Edward, he had to hurry to keep up with his friend as he marched toward the darkened rose garden. The path narrowed as it wound among the flower beds. Everyone else had gathered around the refreshment tables that had been set up near the reviewing stand and the bower of roses looked deserted.

They were almost ready to turn back when suddenly they heard Cecily cry, "Let me go! I'll scream if you—" Her last words were so muffled as if someone had put a hand over her mouth.

With a savage oath, Edward dove through the shrubbery into the secluded arbor. Chandler followed and saw Cecily struggling in Basil Dudley's arms as the actor tried to plant a kiss on her mouth. Chandler, knowing all the hours Edward had spent sparring at Jackson's and wanting him to be the one to save Cecily, made no move to help him.

Edward sent the actor sprawling with one blow. "Stand up, you damned blackguard!" he challenged as his fists knotted, obviously itching to throw another punch.

"You cut my lip," Dudley whined, making no move to rise from the ground. "How am I going to perform tomorrow?"

"You'd best worry if you're going to *live* until tomorrow!" Edward warned before turning to the woman sobbing at his side. As furious as his voice had been, it was now lovingly concerned as he asked, "Cecily, are you all right? Did he hurt you?"

"Oh, Edward, it was so awful. He tried to—Oh, I can't tell you," she cried, casting herself into his arms. "Just hold me...please."

Edward's embrace tightened. He dropped a light kiss on her golden curls, then gently put her away from him. He looked down at the actor who was getting cautiously to his feet. "Now you're going to pay a bloody good penalty for this night's work, Dudley!"

The actor retreated several steps and threw out his hands. "Look, Maitland, if you want to flatten someone, better make it Sir Wilbert. This was all his idea and I was a mutton-headed fool to let that toad talk me into it."

For the first time Chandler took a hand in the matter. "Sir Wilbert Wythe? Giles's cousin? What does he have to do with this?" He took two menacing steps nearer the cowering actor. "You'd better tell us everything or I'll take a swing or two at you myself."

Obviously desperate to shift the blame, Dudley explained hurriedly. "Sir Wilbert is deep in dun territory. He thought if he embroiled Lady Wythe's family in a messy scandal, the *ton* would shun her and she might be more willing to listen to his suit."

"So you were supposed to seduce Cecily?" Chandler demanded.

"The chit seemed willing enough. Why not?"

"And no doubt Sir Wilbert promised you a fat slice of any fortune that fell his way if you helped, didn't he? What a stupid plan! Lady Wythe would never have married that cur. I wouldn't have let her!"

"I told him I didn't believe it would work," Dudley

claimed, eyeing Edward's clenched fists nervously, "but he really didn't care. Sir Wilbert said, whether Lady Wythe married him or not, at least he'd have his revenge for what he called her high-flown airs. There's Sir Wilbert now," he yelled, gesturing to a dim figure hovering behind them. "Go take your fists out on him."

The actor's voice had apparently carried to Sir Wilbert because he hastily began to skulk away toward the dark shadows. In a bound, Edward was after him. Wilbert whirled around suddenly and the blade of a knife flashed in the dark. Cecily's scream reached Chandler a moment before Wilbert lunged.

Edward twisted aside and brought his fist crashing down on Wilbert's wrist. The blade clattered to the ground. Edward grabbed it quickly. Holding it poised at Wilbert's heart, he vowed, "I would hate to be the death of one of my intended wife's relatives, even one who's as remotely connected as you are, but if you ever again cause trouble for anyone in the Millbourne family, I swear I'll come after you. Nowhere will be safe." He snapped the blade shut and let it drop. "Now get away from here!"

As Wilbert scurried off, Cecily looked shyly up at her savior. "Edward," she sighed, a rosy blush coloring her face, "you hadn't said anything...I mean...Do you really want to marry me?"

He smiled down at her. "This was hardly the way I planned to ask you, but there's nothing in the world I would rather do."

"This must be the day for coming up to scratch," Chandler remarked as he joined them. Perhaps it can be a double wedding." He chuckled. "Adrian called this afternoon to ask for Lucinda's hand. Now all we need to do is settle the older sister. Where do you suppose Rosanna is? She's missed all the excitement."

CHAPTER
Ten

WHILE THE FATES or her sisters was being happily settled in St. James's Park, Rosanna's impulsive decision was bringing her nearer the address on Basil Dudley's invitation. The house on Tamberly Street was located in a narrow side street near Berkeley Square. Candles blazed at every window, assuring her that a party was taking place inside. Convinced Cecily must be there, Rosanna mounted the steps and rang the doorbell.

It all looked most proper until the door slammed shut behind her and a huge man, who must have spent a goodly amount of time in the ring as a pugilist, moved to block any possible exit. "Well, dearie, it's about time you got here!" a woman shrilled as she grabbed Rosanna's arm. "Let me look at you."

Stunned, Rosanna didn't resist as the coarse woman, with bobbing curls of an improbable red, made her turn around for an inspection. "You'll do, dearie! My name's Mavis. I suppose Miss Ruby sent you. I declare, she's fashioning herself a group of elegant ladies this season, isn't she now? Well, she's been in the business as long as I have and knows your type appeals to some men. But we're going to have to do something about that bosom."

Before Rosanna could protest, the woman grabbed her bodice, loosened the lacings, and yanked down the fabric until the neckline rested at the very edge of her breasts' rosy peaks. "There, that's better." The woman's harsh laugh grated out. "You may be playing the lady this evening, dearie, but even a pretend lady has to look like a woman!"

"There is a misunderstanding here," Rosanna pleaded, casting uneasy glances at the brute guarding the door. "I'm here to find my sister."

"Ah, a family business, is it? Well, she's bound to be in the dining room. The fun's just about ready to start in there, so you'd best hurry."

Rosanna wondered nervously what type of party she'd walked into. This was certainly different from the routs she'd attended in Somerset. Then happily an answer occurred. Perhaps it was a costume fete. Yes, that must be it. She'd heard of balls where everyone dressed as shepherds or beggars. These were probably friends of Dudley's from the theater, so of course their manner and dress would be a bit odd. They were no doubt all attired as characters from plays. Her glance flickered distastefully over the hostess. Mavis was apparently garbed as some vulgar bar maid out of Chaucer. Well, Rosanna vowed silently, adjusting her bodice upward to a more proper level, she wasn't playing the role of a trollop!

Following the hostess to a chair along one side of the long banqueting table, Rosanna decided with relief that the scene in the dining room looked tame enough. True, the other women were sporting too much rouge and lip tint for her taste, but, she reminded herself, they were actresses. "I'm not here to dine," Rosanna insisted as an old gentleman arose and pulled out the chair next to him. "I would like to go and search for my sister."

"Oh, are there two of you lovely young ladies?" the man asked, sending his watery eyes slithering over her body. "You've outdone yourself, Mavis!" His smile smoothed out some of the wrinkles pleating his face, but it did nothing to make Rosanna feel any easier. Shivering, she decided she most definitely didn't like his smile. It was coldly hard and amazingly intimidating.

Before she could protest taking a seat next to this unsavory roué, he demanded, "Mavis, fetch this lady's sister. I've a mind for two companions this evening."

Mavis began to argue, then shrugged resignedly. "Oh, very well, what does the chit look like?" she asked, pushing Rosanna forcefully down into the chair. "I'll bring her."

"She's about eighteen, with blond hair and blue eyes. She'll be in the company of Basil Dudley, the actor."

"Dudley? Well, that should make for a bang-up evening!" A coarse chuckle followed this observation as Mavis moved away.

At least this was a way to find Cecily, Rosanna mused, for she'd already determined that the house had many rooms filled with revelers. Her thoughts were interrupted when her dining partner pressed an unwanted glass of wine into her hands. He spoke a few commonplaces and his words were polite, but his gaze was not. Rosanna shuddered, feeling that his wandering inspection was mentally stripping the clothing from her body. A large gulp of wine fortified her enough to hide her revulsion. Why didn't that woman return with Cecily?

Luckily the man at her side was distracted when the band began to play a throbbing gypsy song. With a loud yell, a black-haired woman leaped up on the table and began to dance. Her high-kicking steps sent plates and wine goblets smashing to the floor as the wild melody grew savagely louder. Rosanna glanced around the table, stunned that no one seemed even to notice the flying crockery. Everyone's attention was riveted on the whirl-

ing dancer. Glancing at the men around her, Rosanna
shivered again when she saw the undisguised lust burning
in their eyes. Their clapping hands beat a passionate
rhythm, urging the dancer to greater frenzy. With her
hair whipping about her body, the gypsy went into a mad
whirl as the music pounded louder. Her colorful skirt
flared higher and higher until, with a gasp, Rosanna
realized she was wearing nothing underneath!

Her chair crashed backward as Rosanna sought to
escape the lewd insanity filling the dining room. She
started instinctively for the front door. Speeding around
the corner, she crashed into Chandler.

"Thank God I found you!" The words sounded like
they were wrenched from his heart. Leaning toward her,
Chandler whispered rapidly, "Say nothing! For once use
your head and follow along with my game."

Confused, she glanced back over her shoulder and
saw Mavis and the older man, who'd looked her over so
insultingly, coming out of the dining room after her.
Chandler wrapped a firm arm around her waist and pulled
her hard against his body. "Sorry, old chap, but this
ladybird is mine. I saw her on the boards at Covent
Garden and left word backstage for her to meet me here."

"Preposterous!" The older man quivered indignantly.
"I thought she was promised to me! Can't you have the
chit another night?"

"I believe this gracious lady can secure you another
wench to bed." Chandler dangled a plump pouch toward
Mavis. "After all, one doxy's much like another in the
dark."

Rosanna nervously noted the skeptical look in the
woman's eye and feared she'd reject the purse, but the
tempting jangle of gold sovereigns decided the issue. "So
you're an actress?" Mavis observed, taking the bag
greedily from Chandler. "I thought you were from Ru-

by's stable of fillies, but this is better. We won't have to split the take, will we, dearie?" she cackled. Then her sharp eyes narrowed dangerously. "I'll be watching. You'll have to pleasure this fine big man well to claim your share of these coins. I've got my reputation to consider."

Turning to the rejected man, she soothed, "Come, my friend. If I recall, actresses never were your favorite pieces anyway. I've got something better for you stashed away in the mirrored chamber upstairs. Just in from the country and fresh as a daisy, if you take my meaning." She poked him knowingly in the ribs before leading him toward the stairway.

The instant they were alone, Rosanna pleaded, "Chandler, please help me find Cecily so we can get out of this horrible place. These people frighten me!"

"As well they should!" he muttered savagely. "You little fool, don't you know this is the infamous Hellfire Club you've wandered into?"

Rosanna's breath caught in horror at his words. Even in Somerset rumor of the evildoings at London's Hellfire Club had been whispered about. She clung closer to Chandler, trying unsuccessfully to stifle a shudder of fear. "What are we going to do? Cecily's here with that awful Dudley." Her voice rose in panic. "We have to find her, to rescue her! What if he's already—"

A hard kiss muffled the rest of her words. Chandler raised his head until their lips were a mere breath apart. "Stop this foolishness instantly!" he whispered harshly. His arms felt like iron bands as they held her tightly against him. "I warn you, we are both in danger if they discover we aren't who we pretend to be. I'll explain everything if you'll keep a lock on your chatter. Promise?"

"I promise."

Chandler's grasp relaxed as his mouth descended to claim hers again. This time his intent wasn't to muffle her words. His touch was gently reassuring as his kiss softly caressed away some of her trembling fears. When he pulled back again, he explained in a low voice that only she could hear, "Rosanna, we're in a lot of danger. Believe me, these people wouldn't hesitate to dump my dead body in the Thames and I don't even want to think what might happen to you. That red-haired harpy is already suspicious. Even though I've never frequented this place, they're bound to know who I am. Worse, they'll know I'm an active member of the House of Lords. There's talk in Parliament of closing down these establishments. She may think I'm here to gather evidence, that they'd do anything to keep from becoming public. Trust me. I must seem to be besotted with you and you must play my willing light-skirt if we ever hope to get out of here."

"Chandler, surely you're exaggerating!" Rosanna argued as he led her to a sofa upholstered in maroon velvet. When he reached across her to dim the lamp next to them, she saw it was decorated with naked golden cherubs entwined in most suggestive positions. "They wouldn't..." Her words faded as she remembered the menacing stance of the huge man guarding the door. Obviously he was there to keep people from leaving. Suddenly she knew with awful certainty that Chandler wasn't spinning a tale. That meant Cecily was in even more danger than she was!

"How are we going to find Cecily?"

"Shhh," Chandler scolded as his fingertips caressed the full curve of her lower lip. His kiss took her mouth for a moment, then he nibbled a leisurely path to her ear. His warm hand caressed the sensitive side of her throat. "Close your eyes and listen. I'm going to act as if I'm seducing you. At least pretend to enjoy it," he commanded in an undertone. "Your sister isn't here. She never was."

Rosanna sighed when she heard that. Whether it was from relief or the vastly disturbing effect the words blown into her ear were having on her emotions, she wasn't sure. Chandler continued toying about her ear and the back of her neck as he whispered the rest of the story about Cecily's rescue, Edward's declaration of love, and Wilbert's rout.

The details of the story became more and more foggy as the touch of his mouth, the warmth of his breath, and the caress of his fingertips slowly built a fire within her. Rosanna's gentle hands pulled Chandler's face around so she could look at him. She knew her eyes were dark with desire, but she didn't lower her gaze. Before all sanity was gone, she had to know everything. "Cecily's really safe?"

"Yes, far safer than you are. While I was prying the story about Dudley's rendezvous and the invitation to this hellish place out of that damned actor, Adrian, Lucinda, and Lady Kittering arrived. At last sight, your repentant sister had cast herself onto Edward's chest and was proceeding to ruin his new coat with her tears. The damned fool didn't seem to mind at all. Now it's you I'm concerned about."

"Well," Rosanna murmured, winding her arms unashamedly around his neck, "as I recall, you're to be besotted, and I'm to play the light-skirt. I haven't had much experience seducing a man, but I'm willing to try."

Chandler sat still, letting her run her fingertips across the chiseled planes of his face, up to tangle in his golden hair, then down to caress his mouth. He parted his lips and pulled one of her wandering fingertips into the warm interior. Rosanna's breath came quicker as his tongue rasped along the sides, before his teeth closed for playful nips. At last he released his willing prisoner. "Kiss me, Rosanna," he urged in a husky voice.

She felt the heat rising in her face, but she didn't resist. Her hands slid under his frock coat to find the powerful beat of his heart. The garish decorations of the room, the danger they were in, even her concern for Cecily, faded into unimportance. She nestled closer in his arms until her breasts were crushed against him. Her hands had found their way to the back of his powerful neck to force his head down to meet her waiting mouth.

The touch was more explosive than anything Rosanna had ever experienced. At the first sensation of his tongue stroking across her lips, they parted eagerly to welcome his plundering invasion. She arched instinctively against him, snuggling deeper into his embrace. His exploring tongue met an answering thrust from hers as they exchanged pleasure for intimate pleasure.

Finally Chandler pulled away from the drugging sweetness of her mouth. Rosanna's eyes, glazed from the passion they'd shared, fluttered open. His gaze, burning hotly, never left her face as he eased her away from him just enough to find and caress her breast. It seemed so natural, so right, so inevitable, that she didn't try to wrench away but instead savored the deepening ache of desire that spread through her body. She felt the lacing of her bodice fall free and the first questing touch of his caress against the rosy peaks of her breasts. "I think you're enjoying this," she murmured, so bemused she hardly knew she'd spoken.

"As you are, Rosanna," he retorted gently when her peaks hardened and thrust against his palm. "I warned you that one day your impetuous nature would lead you into trouble. Perhaps next time you'll think before you go dashing off to rescue your sisters." He bent to kiss the full curve of her breast that had been exposed by his exploring hands.

"Would you have expected me not to try to help Cecily when I thought she was in danger?" she asked, trying to think coherently.

"No, I know you too well for that!" He chuckled. "Your spirit is one of your most attractive qualities. It reminds me of Bucephalus's stubborn streak. As I've said before, it's a challenge. As much of a challenge as getting you out of here."

"How are you going to do it? From what that horrible woman said, you're supposed to, ah, enjoy yourself here," Rosanna stammered.

"I couldn't enjoy myself here if I'd been on a desert island for five years!" Chandler vowed with obvious disgust. "This place is bloody awful! It will cost a pretty penny, but I may be able to buy your way out of here." His eyes caressed her breasts one last time before he gently instructed, "Lace your bodice, Rosanna, while I tell Mavis I wish to take you home to my own bed, instead of enjoying such delights as the mirrored chamber she mentioned before."

With pretended unconcern, Rosanna leaned back into the corner of the maroon sofa and slowly, teasingly, began to relace her bodice. Mavis's hard eyes were on her. For a few dreadful moments longer, she had to play Chandler's eager doxy while he bought their way out of the Hellfire Club.

It took another fat pile of gold sovereigns before Mavis motioned the loutish guard away from the front door. Rosanna knew that until they were safe in the carriage the game could still be lost. They must not seem in a hurry to escape. Putting a most suggestive wiggle into her walk, she approached Chandler. She stopped close in front of him, smiled as provocatively as she knew how, then wound her slender arms around his neck and gave him one more lingering kiss. His touch fired her blood as he tasted her willing lips.

When he pulled away, he winked at the red-haired procuress. "I believe this chit will be worth every one of those gold coins!" The woman's crude laughter followed them as they finally made it through the doorway to freedom.

Chandler's faithful groom leaped from the driver's seat the instant he saw them approaching and threw open the carriage door. "Praise be, ye got the lassie out of that wicked place! Thought I might have to call on the Iron Duke to rescue the both of you!"

"Don't spare the horses. I want us away quickly!"

Chandler helped Rosanna into the carriage then quickly climbed in after her. As the groom slammed the door shut, Chandler wrapped his arms tightly about Rosanna. Her trembling slowly ceased as she nestled securely in his embrace. With a sigh, she cuddled her head against his shoulder and savored the trusting safety she found in his strong arms. The groom took Chandler's orders to heart and sent the carriage careering rapidly through the quiet streets of Mayfair toward Grosvenor Square. Rosanna didn't mind the swaying and jarring since Chandler was there, holding her close.

They were nearing Chandler's town mansion when he chuckled. Rosanna raised her head and sought his smile in the dim interior of the carriage.

"What's so amusing? It's scarcely a laughing matter to be trapped in such a dreadful place. You didn't even get to see the gypsy who was dancing in the most scandalous manner you can imagine! I'm sure the blush will permanently tint my face!"

"Well, consider it this way, Rosanna. You'll have a very exciting story to tell your grandchildren. Besides, you're most attractive when you blush."

"You still haven't told me what you found so amusing."

He pulled her more firmly onto his lap. "I was merely remembering how admirably you played the role of my willing light-skirt. I had no idea you were such an accomplished actress. Perhaps you should try your luck on the boards at Covent Garden. Or perhaps I should have a go at the theater as well, since we both played our parts this evening with such abandon. We could form a team and do plays from Molière, then move on to—"

The rest of his teasing was lost as the truth of his words stabbed through to Rosanna's heart. Acting a part, that's what he'd thought she'd done. That's what *he* had done. Deep inside she knew that her passion, her desire, her compelling need for his touch, weren't part of an act. No, they were all too real!

The truth was hard to face, but she could no longer deny it. What had happened on that sofa—indeed, what had happened when he evoked her passion at Hampton Court—was no accident, no pretense! She'd given her kisses, her caresses, her passion, willingly and eagerly because she was in love with him. Even the secrets beneath her bodice had been offered with no shame. She loved Chandler! That blinding face echoed painfully through her mind.

Rosanna mentally lashed herself with the cruel truth. Chandler was the one who'd been acting. To him, the passion was a sham, merely a ruse to get her out of the trap she'd foolishly fallen into. No doubt he'd enjoyed the whole experience enormously, enjoyed playing a scene where he could steal a few meaningless caresses.

The carriage rumbled to a stop. With a savage wrench, Rosanna threw herself from his arms. Swallowing back the tears that were threatening to choke her, she thrust open the door. "I'm glad you think I make such a splendid doxy!" she cried.

No backward glance interrupted her flight into the house and up to the lonely privacy of her bedchamber.

CHAPTER
Eleven

SOBBING, ROSANNA FELL across the bed and buried her head in her arms. She didn't hear the door open. Suddenly strong, battle-hardened hands flipped her onto her back. Chandler's thundering frown blazed down at her. "Hell and damnation, Rosanna, what did you mean by that foolish display? Are you overset because I called you a light-skirt? Since when have you put on such missish airs?"

"Get out! Get out of my bedchamber!"

Chandler's powerful hands easily held her prisoner. "Not until you tell me what set off this idiotic screech."

Rosanna struggled to push him away. Furious that he wouldn't leave her to sob her shame out in peace, she swung her small fists hard against his broad chest. With a muffled oath, he effortlessly grabbed both her hands in one of his and pulled them above her head.

"Damn it, Rosanna, tell me what's wrong before I really lose my temper!"

Tears filled her eyes. Humiliated, she twisted her head away so he couldn't see her anguish. But without her meaning it to, the truth escaped. "Giles's kisses were mere pretense as he seduced me into his bed. Learning that hurt more than you can ever know. I thought better of you." Her tears fell unheeded to the pillow beneath her head. "But I was wrong."

With his free hand, Chandler forced her head back so that she was forced to look at him. She couldn't though. The betrayal was easier to endure if she couldn't see his handsome face, couldn't see the blue eyes she'd come to love. Salty tears trickled down her cheeks, making a cold, wet path. "Rosanna, look at me, please look at me." She didn't want to obey, but there was a hint of wistfulness in his words that made her eyes flutter open.

"I lied tonight when I said I was going to pretend to seduce you. Far from pretending, my intentions were quite serious. Believe me! I want you to warm my bed, and that isn't a lie. The moment I found out from that foul actor where you'd gone, I decided the only way to keep you from impetuously tearing off into more danger was to keep you by my side, both day and night. Then at least I'd know you were safe. Rosanna, I'm a soldier, not some *tonnish* dandy! I've had enough of these courting games. It was all I could do not to take you on the grass at Hampton Court and make you mine. I even tried staying away from you, but I couldn't! I'm through being noble. Tonight I have no intention of resisting the passion you stir in me."

He spoke not one word of love, her heart cried. Not one word of any feeling other than desire; desire identical to the urges that sent Giles's rutting in the hay with his bit of muslin. More tears gathered. Why did she have to fall in love again with such a man! She had nothing left now but pride. But pride would at least allow her the dignity of refusing him her ultimate surrender.

Rosanna bravely blinked back the tears and looked defiantly into his eyes. "You claim you like a challenge. Is it a challenge to force your attentions on a woman who doesn't want them, on a woman who despises your touch? Where's the sport in that? You're stronger than I am. You can have your way. I can't stop you."

"Who's lying now, Rosanna? You don't despise my touch. Besides, I have no intention of forcing anything on you. Those were brave words, milady, but your kisses tell me the truth. We've struck sparks of passion since the first day I walked into that study and encountered the stormy depths of your gray eyes. I've given up trying to understand the effect you have on me. Tonight I intend to enjoy the power you possess, the power you have to excite me beyond all reason. And you, my lovely lady, shall enjoy it, too."

"Never!"

A slow smile spread across his face. "We shall see," he murmured, lowering his head.

She struggled helplessly to escape, but he held her gently but firmly down on the bed. All she could do was turn her head away, guessing he would try to capture her mouth.

But Chandler didn't move so directly. Instead, with feather-light strokes he began to kiss the tears from her face. His touch caressed her cheeks, the damp path to the shell of her ear where one bitter drop had strayed, her moist eyelashes, the corner of her mouth. Her fingers clenched, desperately willing her body not to respond to the passion he was kindling. But it was impossible.

With effort, she kept her face averted. But that only succeeded in baring her throat to Chandler's kisses. A few tears had traced trails down the side of her neck and his searching lips followed. She gasped when she felt the soft rasp of his tongue licking away the salty evidence of her pain. Even after the last trace of her tears was kissed away, his sweet torment continued. The pleasurable ache continued to spread, heating her blood, demanding a satisfaction she knew only one man could provide.

Chandler slipped down beside her on the bed. His

muscled leg rubbed slowly, tantalizingly, against her thigh, exciting the stirring need to a new intensity. Then he moved his leg across her body, warmly pinning her more completely beneath him. Keeping her hands most effectively imprisoned, he stopped kissing her, watching instead the rapid rise and fall of her chest. Rosanna fought to control her breathing, knowing only too well how the ragged breaths pushed her breasts invitingly up against the thin silk of her sapphire gown.

Skillful fingers began slowly undoing the lacings of her bodice. His kiss followed as each new area of skin was bared to his touch. Rosanna heard his sharp intake of breath when, for the second time that evening, her softly rounded breasts swelled from her discarded bodice. His firm lips started laying butterfly light kisses across the sensitive peaks. She willed her senses not to feel, not to respond, but still couldn't muffle the moan of desire that escaped when he began to tease her nipples with his tongue.

"Chandler, please!"

He lifted his head. "Please what, Rosanna? Plese stop? Or are you wanting, needing, our lovemaking as much as I am?"

"Blast you!" she cried, but her eyes pleaded with him.

His fingers stroked across her cheeks. "Why are you so angry with me? Or is it yourself, your own body, your own desires, you claim to despise?" He released the gentle hold that had kept her hands prisoner. Softly he stroked down to cup the heavy curve of her breasts. "Do you still want me to get out? I've never known you to lie, Rosanna. Tell me you don't want this to happen tonight."

"I can't."

The words of her defeat were so softly uttered that he

had to bend to hear them, but then a boyish smile flashed across his face. As always she couldn't resist the pull of that smile. An answering one curved up her lips. "Ah, that's better," he teased, brushing a light kiss across her mouth.

Then he captured her hands again and pressed a kiss on each wrist. "Forgive me for forcing your surrender, but I didn't know any other way to make you listen to me."

"I was afraid to listen because I knew that if I did, we would end the evening in each other's arms."

"It wouldn't have made any difference. Our being together like this was inevitable. Whether we shared love tonight, tomorrow, or next week, it would have happened some time." He traced a finger along the soft curve of her chin. "You know, I think it was the defiant tilt of this stubborn little chin that first attracted me. When I meet most women, they eagerly cast all sorts of lures my way, but not you." He settled her more closely into his arms. "It intrigued me that first afternoon when you wished me to the devil, then later came down for our gallop dressed in an old habit with your hair tied carelessly back in a ribbon."

Rosanna's hands, entwined in his blond hair, gave a gentle yank. "I think that's a hum. You seemed far from intrigued that day as you threw your preference for fair-haired chits up to me!"

He buried his face in her lilac-scented curls. "In the first place, if I recall, I was a bit angry when I said that, and besides, until I met you my taste did run decidedly in that direction. But a man can change his mind."

He started to claim her mouth, but she held him off. "What about Lady Pondesbury? You seemed most enamored of the lovely widow."

"There's only one lovely widow I'm enamored with, and she's lying beside me right now.

"That doesn't answer my question."

"I don't suppose I'm going to get a kiss until I explain, am I?" When she shook her head, he continued, "I won't deny that Elvinia and I had a flirtation before I met you, but I discovered quickly what a selfish person she is. When you came to London, I must confess squiring her seemed an ideal way to pique your jealousy. After all, I thought you had that blasted Adrian sitting in your pocket!"

She touched his firm mouth. "Adrian's heart belongs to Lucinda. It always has. He's just a friend."

"I know that now, but at the time watching him touch you nearly drove me into a towering rage. I wanted you, all of you, to myself," he murmured before stroking a trail toward her waiting lips.

Before tasting of her sweetness, he moved so that she lay more intimately beneath him. His obvious desire aroused intense longing within her. The time was past for soft kisses. An exploding need drove their mouths hard together. There was no hesitation as Rosanna opened her lips willingly to take the thrust of his tongue. Stroke after velvety stroke inflamed them. Slowly he withdrew his touch. Her tongue followed until, with a moan, she allowed him to pull it into his mouth. Never had she taken such a lead in lovemaking before, but the wondrous power she had to arouse him swept away all restraint.

With obvious effort, Chandler pulled away from her seductive enticement. "I don't—" His voice was so hoarse, he had to start again. "I don't think you need a maid tonight, do you?" His eyes burned hot. "I want to undress you. I want you to do the same for me. Will you?"

Her only answer was to reach up and start undoing the starched cravat around his neck. It was an action that drew a deep, contented chuckle from him. When the cravat was discarded, Chandler rolled off Rosanna and pulled her to her feet beside the bed.

With loving hands, he slipped the sleeves of her gown down her arms, then released the tie at the waist. The silk fell in a pool of sapphire about her feet. He took a step back and waited.

Rosanna's fingers trembled slightly as she worked at the buttons of his coat, then his waistcoat. His shoulders appeared even broader when these garments followed the cravat to the floor and only the thin white linen shirt remained. The heat of his body flowed through the fabric to warm her hands as she eased the shirt from his body. The blond hair curling across his chest lured her. She delighted in the sensuous prickling of her fingertips as she trailed caresses through the thick mat.

Chandler's hand reached up to still her explorations. His voice was thick and husky with wanting. "Your touch is more intoxicating than the finest French brandy. It fills my senses and clouds my intentions. I want tonight to be beautifully satisfying for both of us." He smiled crookedly. "So I warn you, if you continue those bewitching caresses, we'll end up in a tumble on the floor with you still in that petticoat." He moved closer, spanning her waist until his fingers found the ties of her slip. "And while that is a most attractive petticoat, I'm greedy tonight. I want to see all of you." With a soft yank, the sash came loose.

Chandler turned away for a moment to shrug out of his remaining garments. Rosanna, likewise, let the last coverings fall to the floor. She was belting the sash of her wrapper when his eyes returned to her. "No, that won't do. Please come to me. I need you in my arms, but when you come, I want nothing between us."

Rosanna let her eyes travel over the expanse of his body, from his broad shoulders to the muscular power of his legs, then up again to lose herself in the blue depths of his eyes. He was, as she'd known from the very first, a magnificent man. And he was right. This moment had been inevitable since her father's will had pulled him into her life. It didn't matter that he hadn't said a word about love. She was his. All of her belonged to him, her heart and her body. There was no hesitation, no trembling of her fingers, as she untied the sash of her wrapper and let it drop to the carpet.

Chandler's gaze never left her as he reached behind him and pulled back the covers. "Isn't it wonderful that the night contains so many long hours?" he whispered, taking her hand and drawing her down beside him on the bed.

Slowly pleasure built on top of exquisite pleasure. Kiss followed kiss, caress followed caress, until every nerve in her body was sensuously demanding the final embrace. Even then, even when they were one, the slow savoring continued, driving her to ecstasies she'd never before experienced.

Long moments later, Rosanna lay cuddled in his warm embrace. Chandler tangled his fingers in her long hair and gently brought her face near. "It's never been that beautiful, that completely satisfying, for me."

The depth of feeling in his words reached out to her. She knew he wasn't lying. Leaning down, she kissed him. "You said the same words that were on my lips." A smile softened her mouth. "I'm glad we waited. I can't deny that the temptation was powerful, but that grass at Hampton Court was damp, to say nothing of the possibility of being interrupted." Her kiss stroked lingeringly over his lips again. "It's nice that we know there won't be any interruptions tonight."

"Is that an invitation for futher dalliance, Rosanna? What a bold vixen you've become!"

"Only your touch has the power to make me this bold."

With a chuckle, Chandler began stirring the fire in her blood again with his delightful caresses. It wasn't until the weak light of dawn was beginning to filter into the room that they finally fell asleep.

Much later Rosanna stretched sleepily. Her outflung foot encountered the furry expanse of Chandler's leg. Teasingly, she rubbed her toes up and down, gradually waking him. With his eyes still closed, he reached out and drew her close against him. "I can't think of anything more perfect than to wake up every morning with you beside me like this."

Finally his eyes opened and he smiled at her. With provocative slowness, he eased the silk sheet from her body. "Ah, just as I thought. You're as beautiful in the daylight as by flickering candlelight. In fact, I think I may enjoy you even more this way . . . if that's possible."

The touch of his kiss was as wonderously exciting as before. Rosanna wound her arms around his neck and pulled him back against the pillows.

"It's a good thing I brought your morning chocolate. That stupid maid would probably have dropped the tray if she'd found this scene."

Lady Kittering's voice jarred through the beginnings of their passion. With a gasp, Rosanna pushed Chandler away and yanked the sheet up around her shoulders.

The man at her side glanced across the room, then laughed. He threw his arm casually about her and nestled her back down against him. She tried to resist, but he wouldn't let her. "How can you laugh?" she demanded, embarrassment turning her face a shade of red as bright as the gowns Monsieur de Montaigne had designed for her.

"You don't know that sparkle in my aunt's eye as well as I do. Unless I'm very mistaken, far from being shocked, she's delighted!"

"I certainly am," Lady Kittering commented, as if she found nothing unusual about finding her nephew in bed with his wards' older sister. "And might I say, it's about time! I didn't know you were such a slow top, Chandler. What took you so long?"

"I never ran into such a challenge before." He grinned and gave Rosanna a kiss on her still very pink cheek.

"How did you . . . I mean, you brought two cups of chocolate," Rosanna stammered. "How did you know?"

"Do you mean, how did I know Chandler spent the night with you?" When she nodded, Lady Kittering explained, "I had finally gotten Cecily to sleep when I heard you running in here, then Chandler following. My dear, I've had a few male callers in my day," she confessed with a roguish grin. "When I didn't hear any footsteps leaving, I knew things were going along just fine! Here, my boy, take this tray while I get Rosanna her wrapper. She's attired perfectly for, ah, shall I say, certain very nice activities, but definitely not for sipping chocolate."

Rosanna looked from one to the other and shook her head. If they could be calm about this situation, she supposed she could as well. She took a sip of her hot drink. "Was Cecily terribly upset about that odious Dudley?"

"No more so than she should have been! I believe she has finally learned her lesson about flirting. To be honest, both girls were more overset about your being missing than the dust-up with that actor, but I convinced them

Chandler would take care of you. You must admit, he's obviously doing that rather well! Oh, by the by, when's the wedding?"

Startled, Rosanna glanced nervously at the man beside her. He hadn't said one word above loving her or wanting to marry her. What if he now felt forced to come up to scratch? She couldn't abide having him trapped into proposing. "Lady Kittering, we haven't discussed that yet and I don't think—"

Chandler's hard kiss stilled her words. When he raised his head, he looked anything but trapped. "Will you let me at least propose before you start raising objections?"

"But I don't want you to feel obligated to put a ring on my finger just because your aunt walked in on us and you think my honor is compromised."

"I don't feel the least obligated to do that. My only obligation is to make the woman I love my wife. Rosanna, I'm not spending another night without you in my bed, so we'd better hurry and get that special license or the children will start arriving before the proper nine months. Think of the scandal that would cause! After all, we should set a good example for my wards."

"Are you sure?" she whispered, hardly daring to believe he was saying these wonderful things to her.

"I never knew what love was until you stole into my heart. I've never even said 'I love you' to a woman before. A hundred times I've almost told you how I felt, but I was afraid you didn't return my feelings. I knew you'd been hurt by Giles. You needed time to learn that my words, my love, were true. Last night, when you were in danger, I knew that if anything happened to you, my life would be over as well. I couldn't wait any longer. You ask if I'm sure. I've never been more sure of anything than the depth of the love I offer you."

"Chandler, my boy, that was a very pretty speech.

I've been waiting for you to tell Rosanna that for a vast age. The poor child's been growing quite wan waiting for you to tell her how you feel." Lady Kittering crossed the room toward the door. "That nice Mr. Maitland and your friend Adrian are downstairs paying a call. Thank goodness that young viscount came to claim Lucinda's attention. She was so concerned about you, I was having a devil of a time keeping her out of here. I believe a turn in the park will do your sisters and me good after last night's fracas. No doubt the two gentlemen will be delighted to take us. I'll make sure we're gone for a nice long spell." She winked at them. "Oh, by the way, I told the servants Lady Wythe was sleeping in today and wasn't to be disturbed for any reason."

When Lady Kittering had closed the door firmly behind her, Chandler took the cup from Rosanna's hands and set it on the bedside table. Uncertainty clouded his blue eyes. "I've told you what's in my heart, but you've said nothing in return. I want to believe I taste love in your kisses. Tell me I'm not wrong."

With a tender smile, Rosanna leaned over and gave him one more of those loving kisses. "If I didn't love you so much, I think I'd take offense at that remark. Do you really believe I could love so passionately if I didn't love you with all my heart?" Her smile faded. "No man has ever touched me as you have. It's wondrous. It erases forever whatever I suffered with Giles. Perhaps living through that pain makes love sweeter, more binding, when it finally does come."

"I can't think of anything I'd rather feel than being bound to you forever. Although, I admit that isn't all I'm feeling right now." Gently he began to push the robe from her shoulders. "As my aunt said, a wrapper is fine for sipping chocolate, but not for other activities. I have a few hours before I must leave to get that special license. Can you think how we might spend them?"

With a happy sigh, Rosanna shrugged out of the robe, settled back against the pillows, and held out her arms to enjoy those very nice activities Lady Kittering had mentioned.

All of the above titles are $1.75 per copy

Available at your local bookstore or return this form to:

SECOND CHANCE AT LOVE
Book Mailing Service, P.O. Box 690, Rockville Cntr., NY 11570

Please send me the titles checked above. I enclose _____
Include 75¢ for postage and handling if one book is ordered; 50¢ per book for
two to five. If six or more are ordered, postage is free. California, Illinois, New
York and Tennessee residents please add sales tax.

NAME _____

ADDRESS _____

CITY_____ STATE/ZIP_____

Allow six weeks for delivery.   SK-41

_____ 06692-3 **THE WAYWARD WIDOW** #81 Anne Mayfield
_____ 06693-1 **TARNISHED RAINBOW** #82 Jocelyn Day
_____ 06694-X **STARLIT SEDUCTION** #83 Anne Reed
_____ 06695-8 **LOVER IN BLUE** #84 Aimée Duvall
_____ 06696-6 **THE FAMILIAR TOUCH** #85 Lynn Lawrence
_____ 06697-4 **TWILIGHT EMBRACE** #86 Jennifer Rose
_____ 06698-2 **QUEEN OF HEARTS** #87 Lucia Curzon
_____ 06850-0 **PASSION'S SONG** #88 Johanna Phillips
_____ 06851-9 **A MAN'S PERSUASION** #89 Katherine Granger
_____ 06852-7 **FORBIDDEN RAPTURE** #90 Kate Nevins
_____ 06853-5 **THIS WILD HEART** #91 Margarett McKean
_____ 06854-3 **SPLENDID SAVAGE** #92 Zandra Colt
_____ 06855-1 **THE EARL'S FANCY** #93 Charlotte Hines
_____ 06858-6 **BREATHLESS DAWN** #94 Susanna Collins
_____ 06859-4 **SWEET SURRENDER** #95 Diana Mars
_____ 06860-8 **GUARDED MOMENTS** #96 Lynn Fairfax
_____ 06861-6 **ECSTASY RECLAIMED** #97 Brandy LaRue
_____ 06862-4 **THE WIND'S EMBRACE** #98 Melinda Harris
_____ 06863-2 **THE FORGOTTEN BRIDE** #99 Lillian Marsh
_____ 06864-0 **A PROMISE TO CHERISH** #100 LaVyrle Spencer
_____ 06865-9 **GENTLE AWAKENING** #101 Marianne Cole
_____ 06866-7 **BELOVED STRANGER** #102 Michelle Roland
_____ 06867-5 **ENTHRALLED** #103 Ann Cristy
_____ 06868-3 **TRIAL BY FIRE** #104 Faye Morgan
_____ 06869-1 **DEFIANT MISTRESS** #105 Anne Devon
_____ 06870-5 **RELENTLESS DESIRE** #106 Sandra Brown
_____ 06871-3 **SCENES FROM THE HEART** #107 Marie Charles
_____ 06872-1 **SPRING FEVER** #108 Simone Hadary
_____ 06873-X **IN THE ARMS OF A STRANGER** #109 Deborah Joyce
_____ 06874-8 **TAKEN BY STORM** #110 Kay Robbins
_____ 06899-3 **THE ARDENT PROTECTOR** #111 Amanda Kent

All of the above titles are $1.75 per copy

Available at your local bookstore or return this form to:

SECOND CHANCE AT LOVE
Book Mailing Service, P.O. Box 690, Rockville Cntr., NY 11570

Please send me the titles checked above. I enclose _____ .
Include 75¢ for postage and handling if one book is ordered; 50¢ per book for
two to five. If six or more are ordered, postage is free. California, Illinois, New
York and Tennessee residents please add sales tax.

NAME _____

ADDRESS _____

CITY_____ STATE/ZIP_____
Allow six weeks for delivery.   SK-41